"*I* am *a pirate*,"

Sully reminded her flatly. "And it was you who said all is fair in love and war."

He refused to back down, even as he watched Elizabeth's face fill with disbelief. Perhaps horror.

And one thing he'd realized about Elizabeth—she didn't prevaricate or do things halfway. If she was determined to leave, he had no choice. He had to discard all his scruples to make sure she didn't.

He wanted her to stay.

He wanted her to be his.

He wanted her any way he could get her.

And what Captain Sullivan Fouquet wanted, one way or another, he always got. *Always*. Hadn't he even been brought back from the dead to have his greatest wish fulfilled?

This Valentine's Day, add a little thrill to
your life with four new romances from

Silhouette Romantic Suspense!

This is our first month of new covers to go with
our new name—but we still deliver adrenaline-packed
love stories from your favorite authors.

This month's highlights:

- A doctor and a detective clash when *USA TODAY*
  bestselling author Marie Ferrarella kicks off
  her new series, THE DOCTORS PULASKI, with
  Her Lawman on Call (#1451).

- Meet two captivating characters with a shared past
  in *Dark Reunion* (#1452), the latest in Justine Davis's
  popular REDSTONE, INCORPORATED miniseries.

- Veteran storyteller Marilyn Pappano brings you a
  bad-boy hero to die for in *More Than a Hero* (#1453).

- Voodoo, ghosts and pirates? You'll find them
  all in *The Forbidden Enchantment* (#1454),
  the long-awaited sequel to Nina Bruhns's
  Ghost of a Chance.

Silhouette Romantic Suspense
(formerly known as Silhouette Intimate Moments)
features the best in breathtaking romantic suspense
with four new novels each and every month.

Don't miss a single one!

Nina Bruhns

THE FORBIDDEN ENCHANTMENT

Silhouette®

Romantic

SUSPENSE

This book is dedicated to Diana Downing,
the wonderful bookseller who sold me that first fateful
stack of romance novels…thereby creating a monster.
Thanks, Diana! Without you I'd never have known
what I really wanted to write.

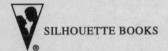 SILHOUETTE BOOKS

ISBN-13: 978-0-373-27524-3
ISBN-10:   0-373-27524-2

THE FORBIDDEN ENCHANTMENT

Copyright © 2007 by Nina Bruhns

Visit Silhouette Books at www.eHarlequin.com

Printed in U.S.A.

Books by Nina Bruhns

Silhouette Romantic Suspense

Ghost of a Chance #1319
Blue Jeans and a Badge #1361
Hard Case Cowboy #1385
Enemy Husband #1402
Royal Betrayal #1424
The Forbidden Enchantment #1454

NINA BRUHNS

credits her Gypsy great-grandfather for her great love of adventure. She has lived and traveled all over the world, including a six-year stint in Sweden. She has been on scientific expeditions from California to Spain to Egypt and the Sudan, and has two graduate degrees in archaeology, with a specialty in Egyptology. She speaks four languages and writes a mean hieroglyphics!

But Nina's first love has always been writing. Drawing on her many experiences gives her stories a colorful dimension, and allows her to create settings and characters out of the ordinary. She has won numerous awards for her previous titles, including the prestigious National Readers Choice Award, two Daphne du Maurier Awards of Excellence for Overall Best Romantic Suspense of the year, five Dorothy Parker Awards and two Golden Heart Awards.

A native of Canada, Nina grew up in California and currently resides in Charleston, South Carolina, with her husband and three children. She loves to hear from her readers, and can be reached at P.O. Box 2216, Summerville, SC 29484-2216 or by e-mail via her Web site at www.NinaBruhns.com or via the Harlequin Books Web site at www.eHarlequin.com.

Dear Reader,

Thanks to all of you who read *Ghost of a Chance* and wrote or e-mailed me asking for Sully's story! Many people have asked me what my inspiration was for doing a pirate tale in a contemporary romance novel. Do any of you remember that fabulous old television series *The Ghost and Mrs. Muir?* Can you say Errol Flynn? Yeah. That about sums it up. Like Tyree's Clara, I've always been a sucker for a pirate. Or should I say privateer?

But seriously, what would a normal (sane!) woman do if she found herself falling in love with a man who thought he was, well, a dead pirate? And worse, one who claimed he'd only come back to life to wreak revenge upon her own family?

I hope you enjoy the story of Elizabeth's dilemma—and the fantasy of being swept away by the man of your dreams.

Take care, and good reading!

Nina

Prologue

1791
An uncharted island just south of Haiti

Never mess with magic.

Playing with things like that could land a man in a world of trouble. And a man's friend, too.

Witches brew, alchemy, love potions, all bad for the soul. And voudou? That was the worst of all.

The night on this island was black as the Devil's heart, lit only by a roaring bonfire and the jaundiced eye of a full yellow moon. Frenzied dancers jumped and swayed to a thumping drumbeat, panting and crying out at crazy visions in their heads. A slow, eerie wind stirred the air.

Christ's Tears. What in God's name were he and Sully doing here?

Captain Tyree St. James watched uneasily as the voudou priest shook some disgusting thing over Sully's head, screaming nasty, garbled words he couldn't understand. Thank the Lord for ignorance. Tyree was just an observer and wanted nothing to do with the whole wretched business.

A reward, Jeantout had said. Jeantout, a leader in the recent slave revolt on Haiti, whose life Tyree and Sully had saved by helping him escape the British army on Sully's ship, the *Sea Nymph*.

The reward? To be initiated into Jeantout's voudou cult; to be granted the power of the curse. Tyree had politely declined.

Sully had accepted. Revenge was a powerful motivator.

Tyree sighed. Sully lived with some powerful demons in his head and heart. Tyree loved his friend like a brother, trusted him with his life every day they sailed in league and would follow him through hell itself. But the man needed to let go of the past.

An involuntary shudder of revulsion sifted through Tyree's body. Aye, he understood well Sully's burning need for revenge. And he'd be the first to take arms and stand by his comrade to rid the earth of the depraved bastard who'd caused his suffering.

But voudou. Voudou had a strange way of twisting itself around a man, invading his own soul rather than fixing the ill it was intended to remedy.

It was a bad business.

Tyree watched his friend accept a grisly rattle-staff

from the voudou priest and hold it high, shaking it with the fury of a man consumed with hatred.

"I curse thee, Lord Henry Sullivan," Sully shouted above the snap of the bonfire and the chanting of the dancers. "I curse you and all you treasure! I pray I live to see the last of your legitimate line die in affliction, swallowed and unremembered by the sands of eternity!"

Good God.

A pretty young thing sauntered up to Tyree, a smile on her lips and a sway to her hips. She plopped down on his lap and put her arms around his neck. "Jeantout, my brother, he say you save his life," she whispered in his ear. "I like to thank you."

Making himself relax, Tyree drew his fingers along her soft cheek. "Oh, aye?"

Now, this was more the reward he had in mind.

She rose, took his hand and led him from the ring of fire, weaving easily through the tumult of dancers. At the edge of the firelight, he turned and took one last look at Sully. A shiver went up his spine, as though someone had just walked over his grave.

A very bad business.

The woman gazed back at him with an enigmatic smile. "Don't worry. Your friend, he get what he want."

"And what is that?" Tyree asked, suddenly wary.

"One day you know," Jeantout's sister said, her sultry eyes glittering. "But now you forget."

And so he did. And he didn't think about Sully's voudou curse again for a long, long time.

Not until the day he woke up dead.

Chapter 1

*Magnolia Cove, Frenchman's Island, South Carolina
June, present day*

He should have stayed dead.

That would have been preferable to this living hell.

Captain Sullivan Fouquet plastered a brittle smile on his face and told himself he must not, under any circumstances, show his pain, or his fear.

Did he say fear? *Non.* More like apprehension. Unease. Nervousness.

Captain Sullivan Fouquet feared nothing in this world. At least not until…

Damnation. Tyree would be able to tell him what to do, how to act. What to be wary of in this strange new time and place and what should be ignored.

Blast the blighter for leaving on his honeymoon now, when Sully needed him most.

"You okay, Chief?"

"Aye," Sully said, gingerly catching the traveling case the man whose name was Jeremy Swift handed down from the huge red conveyance Sully had just descended from himself. "Yes," he corrected himself, and cautiously tested the strength of his weakened knees. That had been quite a ride.

Swift passed him down his walking stick and Sully leaned on it gratefully. No need for his men to know careening down the road in that cursed contraption he'd had his heart in his throat.

"Need help with your bag?" Jeremy asked.

"*Non,* I'm fine." Sully could deal with the pain. It was the strangeness and blind uncertainty he hated.

As proof of his fitness, he turned toward the fancy three-story boardinghouse that was painted the most peculiar green and garnished with white, curlicued latticework. He'd never seen anything quite like it in his life.

His old life.

"This is where you live now, you remember?" Jeremy Swift asked with a slight frown.

"It's coming back to me."

Of course, he'd never seen pretty much *anything* he'd encountered in this extraordinary world since waking from his near-endless slumber. In the hospital Tyree had counseled feigning amnesia to explain his utter lack of recognition of anything around him. As well as why he had none of the memories of the person whose body he now inhabited—Andre Sullivan, a man whose looks were uncannily similar to those of his old self.

"Okay, we'll leave you to it," Jeremy Swift said. "See you tomorrow at the station, Chief."

"Aye," he said, but the word was drowned by the rumbling noise of the giant red fire truck pulling away from the curb. On the side of the truck was emblazoned Old Fort Mystic Fire Department, as were the pockets of the neat blue uniforms of the six smiling men packed inside—*his* men—all waving cheerfully to him as the truck rolled away down the street. A piercingly loud horn blasted twice from the roof of the vehicle, making him cringe, and then it disappeared around the corner.

Leaving him on his own. For the first time in three months. For the first time *ever* since being thrust into this diabolical adventure.

But a coward was something he'd never been, so taking a deep, cleansing breath Sully made himself reach for the gate in the white picket fence surrounding the house's front garden. A neat green painted sign was attached to it. Pirate's Rest Inn.

He gave an ironic smirk.

If they only knew.

"Welcome home, Captain Fouquet," he mimicked in a high voice to the sign. "It's been a long time.

"Aye, two hundred years," he answered himself. "But it's not Fouquet anymore. I'm Chief Sullivan now. Andre Sullivan."

He exhaled. *Non*. No one would be calling him Fouquet, even in error. Sullivan Fouquet had been dead for two hundred years…as they'd continually pointed out in the hospital—until Tyree had convinced him to stop insisting he really was the infamous Cajun pirate captain. Tyree should know—he'd spent two centuries hiding his real identity, even being forced of late to change his name to James Tyler. He said people would start thinking Sully's mind had been mangled along with his body in the fiery accident that had nearly claimed his life.

Alors. The accident that *had* claimed the life of the real Andre Sullivan.

Sully limped a few steps along the cobblestone walkway into the midst of the garden, pausing to take in the incredible array of summer roses blooming along its path. In the hospital, his newly awakened senses had been assaulted by pain and unpleasant smells, tastes and unfamiliar sounds. But now he feasted those abused senses, pulling in deep lungfuls of the fragrance of heavy blooms and warm breeze and fecund earth, teased by distant memories those things evoked.

Mon Dieu, he was alive again!

"Welcome home, Captain. I'm sure you're glad to be out of that awful hospital, eh?" he muttered.

"Aye, I'd nearly forgotten what the world outside looked and smelled like. However, it's Chief now. I'm not a pirate captain any longer, but a fire chief."

Of all things. The mere thought made him break out in a cold sweat. The universe had an oddly perverse sense of humor, it seemed.

If his moldering body had to be resurrected to life, why couldn't it have been as a sea captain? Lying in traction in his cold, narrow hospital bed, his body encased like a mummy in plaster and unable to move, sometimes unable even to blink for the pain of his burns and broken bones, he would imagine himself back on the quarterdeck of the *Sea Nymph,* sailing against the wind, his hair flying and the salt spray in his face. It had been all he could do not to cry out with misery and longing.

"Welcome home, Chief Sullivan," he muttered. "How are you feeling about your terrible ordeal?"

"Like I've just awoken in the broken body of a stranger and have no idea why I'm here."

Tyree said it was because of the curse. The powerful curse Sully himself had shouted in a rage over the death of his beloved fiancée, Elizabeth, when Tyree had shot her.

At the reminder of his sweet lover's demise, Sully's heart squeezed as it always did. In those last years battling the sea and his enemies, Elizabeth had been his shining beacon of happiness, the home port he'd set his compass by. How would he ever bear the coming years without her?

Because he had no choice.

"Welcome back, Chief. Happy to be home again?"

He sighed. "Aye," he answered himself wearily, "thrilled to the core."

"You don't sound very convincing," an amused feminine voice said from the garden.

He spun to the sound, knocking himself off balance. The suitcase dropped from his hand as he struggled to stay on his one good leg. Suddenly she was beside him, grabbing his arm, holding him around the waist.

"Steady there. Sorry! I didn't mean to startle you."

A peculiar tingle sifted through his body, emanating from the places where she touched him.

He stared down at her as his throat tightened. There'd been many women in the hospital who'd touched him. Doctors, nurses, those cute aides in red and white striped uniforms. Even his…that is, Andre's…lady friend Lisa Grosvenor had brushed his cheek with indifferent lips as she'd issued him his sailing orders shortly after he'd regained consciousness.

None of them had affected him. He'd barely even noticed their presence.

But the touch of this woman was…different. Somehow…familiar. Her hand on his waist, even her scent, sweet like the roses surrounding them, with a touch of clove, made his whole being come to life and stand at attention. She reminded him so much of—

All at once, goose bumps roared over his flesh and he lost his breath.

"Elizabeth?"

Startled blue eyes gazed up at him. "Do I…?"

Her words trailed off as he reverently traced her face with his fingertips. *"Mon Dieu.* Can it really be you?"

Her features were not the ones he remembered, her hair a different color. But her scent, her eyes, her touch…a lover did not forget these things.

"Elizabeth?" he whispered again.

"Yes, but…"

With a groan, he folded her in his arms. "Thank God, you're here! I was so afraid I'd lost you forever." He buried his nose in her hair, breathing deeply of her intoxicating scent. "Hold me," he softly said, "so I know you're real."

Hesitantly her arms came around him. The devastating burns on his back had healed for the most part, but he cursed the scars that prevented him from feeling more than the weight of her tentative embrace. He leaned down and kissed the tender spot below her ear, a place she'd always delighted in.

Her body quivered. He rejoiced. *It was her!*

She gave a tiny gasp as he captured her lips with his. He kissed her, gently, savoringly, and she tasted like pure heaven. It had been so long…

Then her arms tightened around him and her mouth opened a fraction. He pulled her close, taking her invitation, kissing her long and deep.

When the kiss finally ended and their lips parted, she whispered, "Welcome back, Chief. Happy to be home again?"

"Aye," he answered with his first true smile since waking from the dead. "Thrilled to the core."

"Well, well, well," a different woman's voice suddenly said from behind him, sarcastic and accusing.

He turned. Lisa Grosvenor stood at the gate, tapping one toe and looking disgusted. "I must say, that didn't take you long. You were discharged, what—" she disdainfully consulted her watch "—all of a half hour ago? And already you've made your first conquest. Or—" she lifted a brow "—perhaps you're old friends?"

"Lisa," he said impassively. He hadn't liked the female the one time they'd met and he liked her even less now. Andre obviously had horrible taste in women. "What do you want?"

Elizabeth disentangled herself from his embrace and backed away, her expression appalled. "You have a *girlfriend?*"

"Had. Apparently. But I have no memory of her, which is probably just as well since she broke it off while I was in the hospital. Didn't like being saddled with a cripple."

"Oh, honestly, Andre," Lisa said evenly. "You act as if it's my fault you're a philandering womanizer. I don't know why I ever thought I could change you. Moving in together was a huge mistake."

He glanced back at Elizabeth, who was still backing away from him. She'd nearly reached the steps of the boardinghouse's broad, wraparound porch.

"Elizabeth, *chère,* wait. I can explain."

With a derisive snort, Lisa walked back to her car and pulled out a cardboard box. "I've brought some of the things I thought you might need. The rest of your belongings are in a storage unit. Address and key are in the box."

"Thanks," he said, but Lisa's attention was on Elizabeth.

"Do yourself a favor, sugar, and don't get involved with Andre Sullivan. He'll fill your heart with pretty fantasies but as soon as he gets what he wants he'll be gone, sure as the sun rises."

"You're the one who left me, Lisa," he reminded her. *Merci, Dieu.*

She gave a final withering glance at Elizabeth. "And not a moment too soon, I see."

With that she stalked to her car, slammed the door and took off.

Jaw clenched, he turned back to Elizabeth. She was on the porch now, eyes wide.

"*You* are Andre Sullivan?"

He blinked. "I'm…" *Dieu.* What should he answer?

"You know who I am, Lizzie." Suddenly he had a terrible thought. "Don't you?"

Her tongue swiped across her lips. She looked stricken. "I, um. I—I'm sorry, I…have to— Oh, God."

She whirled and vanished into the house.

He stood there for several seconds cursing inwardly. Cursing his absurd fate. Cursing Andre's evident reputation as a bounder. Cursing the impossibility of running after Elizabeth because of his shattered body.

But most of all cursing the obvious truth.

She didn't recognize him.

His own woman didn't know who he was.

Elizabeth Hamilton sprinted up the stairs to the cozy room she had rented for her ten-day trip to Magnolia Cove.

What had she done?

Girlfriend or no, she couldn't believe she had let that man kiss her. And kissed him back! A perfect stranger!

She squeezed her eyes shut as she leaned her back against the room's door and twisted the key in the lock.

If only he *were* a real stranger…

But he was *Andre Sullivan,* the very man she had come all the way from Connecticut to South Carolina to find. And not to kiss, either.

This could *not* be happening.

She crossed to the dresser and picked up the framed photo of her family she had placed there—Gilda, Don and Caleb Sullivan—and trailed her fingers over their dear faces. Her parents' best friends, Gilda and Don had adopted her when she was just four, after a drunken driver had killed her real parents and her baby brother. Caleb had been Gilda's late, longed-for blessing, a menopause baby that had taken them all by joyous surprise. Elizabeth had loved him fiercely from the moment she'd seen his pink, squalling face through the hospital nursery window ten years ago, reminding her so much of the baby brother she'd lost.

The year Caleb was diagnosed with leukemia, Don had died suddenly from a stroke.

The doctors had done everything they could to slow the leukemia's progress in Caleb's young body. But what he really needed was an infusion of new bone marrow. Unfortunately compatible donors were proving illusive. Family and friends yielded no match. He'd been on the national bone marrow donor list for three years, with no match in sight there, either.

And now he was dying.

Was everyone she loved destined to be taken from her?

As Caleb wasted away, Elizabeth could only watch in growing panic as she was helpless to stop the death of her beloved brother. Until some old papers she came across mentioned an obscure branch of the Sullivan family that had moved to South Carolina at some point in the distant past.

Finally she could do something! She could track them down and maybe, just maybe, someone in this long-lost branch of the family would prove a match for Caleb.

She'd brimmed with renewed optimism. But to her dismay had discovered after weeks of research that just as in Connecticut, the Carolina Sullivans were nearly extinct. Only one member of the family still survived.

Andre Sullivan.

Caleb's last hope.

Elizabeth decided to avoid Andre for the rest of the afternoon, to allow her roiling feelings to settle. She could hear Mrs. Butterfield, the innkeeper, help him move into his third-floor room, just above her own. Afterward, his uneven gait paced back and forth across the ceiling, floorboards creaking. Was he as restless as she?

Around six, there was a knock on her door and Mrs. Butterfield stuck her head in. "Ten minutes till supper, hon. I've made a special Beaufort stew in honor of Chief Sullivan."

She knew she had to get it together. Avoiding him would not help Caleb.

Still, she hadn't expected to run into him as soon as she walked out of her room a few moments later. But there he was on the landing, resting between floors.

Her pulse kicked up. Too late to retreat now.

"Miz Elizabeth," he said in his delightfully unusual accent that had so charmed her this afternoon…among other things. "I want to apologize for my presumptuousness earlier today. I, uh, mistook you for…someone else. My memory since the accident—" he gave a self-conscious shrug "—it plays tricks."

Her face heated. "Please don't worry about it, Chief Sullivan." She stuck out her hand, determined to be friendly but establish the necessary distance. "Hi. I'm Elizabeth Hamilton."

It wasn't going to be easy. Even leaning on a cane, the man was a stud. Tall, broad shoulders, a face full of character and a killer smile combined into a masculine package any warm-blooded woman could fall for—and apparently did with regularity.

"Enchanté," he said. When his large hand enveloped hers she was surprised by its strength. She could also feel a network of scars crisscrossing the top and calluses on his palm. "Please, call me Sully."

"All right. Sully it is." She started down the stairs.

He gripped the banister and came down after her, one step at a time. When she turned and waited, he tried to hide his pain, but it was evident in the strained muscles of his face.

"My physical therapist insisted my room be on the third floor," he explained apologetically, "in order to exercise my legs. The man's a damned sadist."

"Oh, dear. Let me help you," she said, hurrying back up and offering her arm.

He looked down at it, then at her, and she realized with a rush of heat that a hand on her arm wasn't going to do it. She'd have to put it around his waist to support his weight.

Oh, Lord. Not good.

But she couldn't back down now. She slid her arm around him, trying not to notice how good he smelled, or how well their bodies fit together, even in this awkward position.

She was not here to romance the man, she sternly reminded herself.

When they got to the kitchen, Mrs. Butterfield fluttered about, pointing out their places at the round wooden table, then took a seat herself.

"You two are currently my only guests, so I splurged a little on Chief Sullivan's welcome home supper," she said, beaming at him. "It's such an honor having a hero staying at Pirate's Rest Inn."

"I'm certainly no hero," he demurred. "I only did what any man would have done."

"Well, I'm sure Clara and James Tyler would disagree," Mrs. Butterfield said jovially, bringing over a huge steaming pot from the stove. "Now, dig in, everyone."

Elizabeth had been shocked upon arrival yesterday to learn that Andre…Sully…had been in the hospital for over three months. Not the kind of news she'd wanted to hear about the man she was going to ask to possibly undergo yet another painful medical procedure.

"What happened?" she asked as they dished up, curious to know the details of his heroic deed.

Sully looked reluctant to answer, so Mrs. Butterfield jumped in. "There was a terrible fire in one of the old historic buildings in the village, the Moon and Palmetto pub. Three hundred years old it was. The fire was set deliberately," she said, nodding gravely. "A young couple, the Tylers—they weren't married then, of course— anyway, they had the arsonist cornered in the alley behind the building. Desperate to escape, he stabbed Mr. Tyler badly and shot Mrs. Tyler. Chief Sullivan was dragging her away from the inferno when part of the building collapsed on him. It was a pure miracle all three survived."

Sully stared down at his bowl, picking at a piece of crab. "I just wish the culprit had been caught," he mumbled with a scowl.

"He wasn't?" Elizabeth asked.

"They assume he burned to death," Mrs. Butterfield said. "Very little was left of anything after the blaze was extinguished."

Elizabeth wrinkled her nose. "But surely, his body…"

"Never found," Sully said, then took a big breath and let it out. "But enough of that depressing topic." He lifted a spoonful of the seafood stew they were enjoying, an incredibly tasty broth filled to the brim with shrimp and crab, potatoes, corn and hunks of spicy sausage.

"This is delicious, Mrs. Butterfield," he said with a broad smile. "Reminds me of the gumbo they used to make back home in Louisiana."

"It is wonderful," Elizabeth agreed. And completely different from any New England stews she'd ever tasted. No cream and you had to use your fingers to eat it!

She glanced up and noticed Mrs. Butterfield giving Sully a peculiar look. "But Chief Sullivan, all the newspapers said you were born right here, in the Old Fort Mystic Hospital where you recuperated from your injuries."

Now that she mentioned it… Elizabeth's research had said the same thing. Although, his accent certainly sounded more like Louisiana French than the Charleston drawl she was becoming familiar with.

There was an awkward pause.

He let out a laugh, but it sounded forced. "Yes, of course. I, um… The truth is, when I woke up from my coma I was suffering from a rather fantastical delusion. It occasionally continues to plague me, tripping me up at the most inappropriate times." He darted Elizabeth an uneasy glance.

She knew she really should just nod and smile as Mrs. Butterfield was now doing. But she was from plain-speaking Connecticut, not the über-polite South. His chagrin intrigued her.

"What delusion?" she asked.

For a moment he looked taken aback. Then he forced another laugh. "Truth be told, I had no memory of my own identity. I believed myself to be Sullivan Fouquet. The notorious pirate."

Mrs. Butterfield clucked her tongue in amusement. "I believe I read something to that effect in the papers."

Elizabeth blinked.

Since her arrival yesterday, she had learned a little about the quaint historical village of Magnolia Cove. Located on Frenchman's Island, one of the dozens of small sea islands that crowded the southern coast of South Carolina, it was lush, tropical and all but forgotten by the passage of time. The whole place basked in an atmosphere of lazy, sultry Southern dissolution.

And pirate mania.

Specifically the infamous Cajun pirate, Captain Sullivan Fouquet, who had called Magnolia Cove home while executing his most daring escapades during the late 1700s and the Revolutionary War. In fact, an article in *Adventure Magazine* had recently made the startling revelation that Fouquet had been a patriot, working as a privateer for the American revolutionary forces.

Made famous by the lurid nineteenth-century penny dreadful novel, *The Pirate's Lady,* written by village historian Maybelle Chadbourn, the town had cashed in on its adventurous past in a big way. Shops, restaurants, streets, a museum, the boardinghouse she was staying in and even an annual festival were named in honor of the pirate Fouquet and his swashbuckling cronies.

It was kind of charming, in a kitschy sort of way.

But…good Lord. Sully must have really hit his head hard in that accident.

"Wow," she said, trying not to grin. "Your memory really does play tricks. You honestly thought—"

His brow creased in a fierce scowl, which she suspected was more due to embarrassment than anger. "I'd *prefer* not to talk about it," he growled.

She bit down on the inside of her cheek. "Sure. I understand."

A fire chief who secretly yearned to be a pirate.

For some reason, she found that little bit of absurdity about him unbelievably endearing.

After they finished eating, they retired to Mrs. Butterfield's antique-filled parlor for coffee and conversation—well, mainly Elizabeth and Sully listened to their hostess chatter on about the history of the village, the tourist sights Elizabeth should visit and where Sully might best start his search for a new place to live.

At the reminder of his former girlfriend, Elizabeth shifted uncomfortably. Though why she should care with whom he had lived or not lived, she had no idea.

No, that was a lie. She knew exactly why.

Because of that kiss.

Try as she might, she could not forget the feel of his lips on hers, nor the bald emotion and longing she had felt behind them. She'd never had a man kiss her like that before. The thought of him living with someone else, kissing another woman with such feeling, well, as irrational as it was, it bothered her. How stupid could you get? But damn it, it even made her jealous of the unknown woman he'd mistaken her for!

Who *was* that mysterious woman she'd reminded him of?

Suddenly she recalled a romantic tale she'd read last night in one of the guidebooks on her nightstand. The pirate Sullivan Fouquet had died in a duel with his best friend and partner, fellow-pirate Tyree St. James, after his friend had accidentally shot Fouquet's beloved fiancée, a woman whom, by all accounts, he had loved to distraction.

And her name had been…

Elizabeth.

Chapter 2

Later that night, unable to sleep, Elizabeth was lying in bed thinking about Sully. Why did she have to be so darned attracted to him? Even if he weren't slightly balmy—okay, charmingly so—Lisa Grosvenor's description of him left little doubt as to the kind of man he was. And then there was the reason Elizabeth had come to find him.

She really must keep her distance from Andre Sullivan, for *all* those reasons.

Too bad he was such a wonderful kisser.

A soft knock on her door brought her out of her musings.

"Elizabeth?" Sully's low, masculine voice drifted in from the hall. "You awake, *chère?*"

She sat up in bed, surprised. "Yes… Is there something wrong?"

"Can I come in for a moment?"

She glanced down at her sleep attire—an oversize T-shirt. Not exactly glamorous, but decent enough for company. She slid out and unlocked the door.

He stood there looking rumpled and apologetic, gripping the doorjamb with white-knuckled fingers. "Sorry to disturb you. But—" he grimaced "—I can't seem to make it up to my room without a rest, and there's no seat out here. I saw your light on...."

She quickly moved aside. "Of course, come in." She glanced at the sole chair in the room. It was a squat, deep easy chair that would be difficult for him to rise from once he'd sat down. "Here, sit on the bed," she said, straightening the covers.

He limped over and eased down onto it with a sigh. "*Merde,* I hate being a weakling like this."

"Don't be silly. Healing takes time. You almost died."

"Wouldn't be the first time," he mumbled, set aside his cane and kneaded his thigh with his fingers.

For a reckless second she thought about offering to massage it for him. Then thought better of the idea. Yikes.

"I suppose you face death regularly in your line of work," she ventured, wondering where the heck *she* should sit. The easy chair was in a dark corner on the other side of the room.

"It's a dangerous life," he agreed, working his leg muscles. "Every time you go into battle, you are prepared to die. But this...this is almost worse."

Interesting analogy. She stepped closer, thinking of Caleb facing each day's battle knowing it could be his last. And Sully, choosing to risk his life to save others. They were both so brave. Braver than she.

She had a sudden urge to reach out to Sully, to soothe the frown from his brow. "The pain from your injury must be awful. But surely, the alternative—"

He glanced up and smiled wearily. "Aye. Death is no good substitute. Yet, I'll admit, there have been moments…" His eyes softened, then he looked over his shoulder at the bed. "*Vien,* slide back into bed and relax while I prepare myself for the final ascent." His smile tipped up at the corners. "Or the sight of such pretty bare legs just might give me the notion to linger for reasons other than resting."

Her jaw dropped. Without stopping to think, she scrambled past him onto the mattress and pulled the sheet over her.

He gave her a wry look. "You needn't have moved *quite* so quickly. For future reference, a man's ego is easily bruised."

"I didn't mean—" she started, but he waved her off.

"It's all right. I don't blame you." To her consternation he lifted his leg onto the bed and stretched out full length next to her. "After that scene with Lisa this afternoon. I should explain—"

"There's no need," she assured, watching him uneasily. But he did nothing except wince as he moved his legs into a more comfortable position. "I understand."

"*Non,*" he said, "you do not begin to understand. *Dieu,* how could you? I don't understand any of this myself."

She couldn't help but notice his accent had slipped back into a Cajun patois sprinkled with French words, unlike earlier this evening when he'd made an effort to correct himself anytime that happened. It was weird, but he seemed much more unguarded, more natural, now.

He let out a long breath. "I lost my memory, you know. Everything about myself and the world around me. I didn't remember what cars looked like. How to turn on a television. Or even what it's for. Even now, everywhere I turn there are things I don't recognize."

"It must be tough. Is that why…?" She let her words fade, not wanting to embarrass him again.

"Why I thought I was a pirate who died two hundred years ago, when life was simple and straightforward?" he completed for her. Irony colored his tone, but no discomfiture. "Perhaps."

A warm, humid breeze wafted in from the open window, bringing with it the scent of gardenias from the garden below. Ivory lace curtains billowed lightly, creating intricate patterns that danced on the wall. A soft chorus of frogs croaked in the distance, accompanied by the rhythmic hum of cicadas.

Instinctively knowing she had nothing to fear, she lay down, too, and pulled the sheet up under her arms. For several minutes they simply lay there listening to the sounds of the night.

Then he turned to his side, propped his head on his hand and looked at her searchingly.

My God, he was good-looking. Not in the usual way—he'd never grace the cover of *GQ*. But handsome in the best tradition of a movie bad boy. Really bad boy. Rugged. Intense. Masculine. A touch of danger lurked in the harsh angles of Sully's face. His hair was black as the night, thick and shiny despite the shortness of its hospital cut. He had a strong, square jaw, straight white teeth and sculpted lips that beckoned her to come closer. And his eyes…warm and brown as rich chocolate, ringed with a fringe of dark lashes…contained promises that made her heart flutter madly.

She swallowed.

"Do you believe in reincarnation?" he murmured.

The question threw her. "I, uh…" She refocused her badly flagging attention. "I don't know. Do you?"

His smile was enigmatic. "I didn't used to."

"Sully?"

"Aye?"

"Does this have anything to do with Sullivan Fouquet?"

"Why do you ask?"

"Because you're looking at me funny."

"How, funny?"

Like he wanted to devour her alive, funny.

"Like you know something I don't."

He continued to regard her for a moment in the dim light of the bedside lamp, then his eyes shuttered and he said, "I don't know how I'll do it."

"What?"

"Go on with this life I know nothing about. Andre Sullivan has important responsibilities. What if I can't do them justice?"

"You will," she said. Despite his melancholy, he didn't strike her as a man who would let anything defeat him. "You'll start remembering. And if you don't, you'll learn them again."

He reached out and lightly touched a curl that lay on her pillow. "You just met me. How can you be so sure?"

"Because," she said with a smile, "at dinner you said you were barely alive when they got you to the hospital after your accident. You said at one point on the operating table they even pronounced you dead. But you refused to die. You came back to life. I firmly believe you were brought back for a reason."

"What reason?" he demanded quietly.

"Only time will tell," she said. "But, Sully, I've no doubt you'll know it when you find it."

Revenge.

That was the real reason Sully had come back.

Tyree believed it was because of the same curse that had kept Tyree spirit-bound to his earthly existence for so long. But Sully knew better.

Sully was here because of a different, more powerful curse, taught to him by Jeantout, the voudou prince himself.

He was here to witness the obliteration of the line of his nemesis, Lord Henry Sullivan. Nothing less than that would have had the power to recall him from the grave.

But of course he couldn't tell that to Elizabeth. She would never understand about Lord Henry and the terrible evils he'd wrought upon Sully's family.

So as they lay there side by side in her bed, he asked her about her world. Under the guise of filling in the blanks left by his loss of memory, they talked late into the night.

He felt such an ease of exchange with her it was as

though their relationship had not been interrupted by two hundred years of silence.

And his hunger for her grew by the minute.

He'd wanted her badly, since first seeing her again in the garden. Since that amazing kiss. Being close to her, lying in bed with her like this, made him want her with a yearning that threatened to undo him. But every time he made a move to touch her, she shifted out of reach.

It was making him crazy.

He needed to hold his lover, needed to feel her arms around him and her skin next to his. Needed to taste her and thrust himself deep into her sweet flesh, driving out the lingering spectre of death that still hovered over his psyche.

Couldn't she see, couldn't she sense, that he was her true love, back to reclaim her?

But she thought he was Andre Sullivan. And Sully had begun to discern that Andre Sullivan was not a very nice man. At least when it concerned women. What was it Lisa had called him? A philandering womanizer. *Ouch.* That had always been Tyree's reputation before, not Sully's.

Alors, he just needed to be patient. He must woo Elizabeth to trust him by showing her he wasn't the same old Andre anymore. That he had changed since the accident. More profoundly than anyone would ever suspect.

"Elizabeth?" he whispered after several minutes of silence.

"Hmm?" she answered sleepily.

His blood raced. "May I kiss you good night?"

After a moment she said, "Not a good idea."

He let out a frustrated breath. "Why? Because of this afternoon?"

"Because we hardly know each other."

"We know each other a lot better now than this afternoon," he pointed out. "And you let me kiss you, then."

Another pause. "You caught me by surprise."

"So, if I catch you by surprise again…"

She chuckled softly and turned on her side to face him. "In the garden you said you mistook me for someone else. Who?"

He blinked. *God's teeth.* This was not what he wanted to talk about. Hell, at the moment he didn't want to talk at all. "She was a woman I knew…a long time ago."

"You remember her?"

"I could never forget her."

"Where is she now?"

"She's… She died."

The curiosity in her eyes dissolved to sympathy. "Oh, Sully. I'm so sorry."

"It was your scent that reminded me of her."

Her lips parted. "My scent?"

Unable to help himself, he slid his hand behind her neck and drew her closer. So they were nearly nose to nose.

"Sweet like spring flowers," he whispered. "Spicy like Christmas grog. Warm and alluring like a beautiful woman."

Her nostrils flared and he could sense her skittishness. He wanted to taste her again so badly he was almost willing to take first and ask afterward.

Almost.

"Kiss me, Elizabeth. Kiss me and I swear to you I'll take it no further."

She swallowed and her tongue peeked out and swiped over her lips. He almost groaned aloud.

"Sully, I can't," she whispered. "There's something…some*one* I need to tell you ab—"

His heart roared in protest. "Shh," he swiftly admonished, sorely provoked. *He didn't want to hear it.* He pulled her to his chest. "You have another man. I should have known."

A woman as desirable as she would have men flocking after her. He tamped down his immense frustration, kissed her forehead and forced himself to let her go.

"No, Sully, it's not what you—"

He slid awkwardly out of bed. "*C'est bon.* I should go. We can talk about it tomorrow, *non?*"

Right now he had to get out of there. He was feeling too volatile and she was too tempting.

"Promise?" she asked.

What was he supposed to say? That her being with another man was the last thing he wanted to hear about? "I'm supposed to go into the fire station, but maybe after."

She sat up and hugged her knees. "You're going back to work so soon?"

"They're just having a little welcome home party for me. Though God knows how I'm going to get there. I'm told I own a car, but…" He ground his teeth and reached for the doorknob.

"I'll drive you," she offered.

He turned to regard her. He hated that she was seeing

him like this, weak and pathetically helpless. He was used to being strong and in charge, captain of his ship and master of his world. Invincible.

But he knew pride had its limits, especially around women. Sometimes they even enjoyed taking care of a man.

"I'd be grateful," he said, and he was. "Maybe you can teach me to run the damn contraption."

A grin curved her lips. "I can try."

"All right. See you at breakfast, then."

"I look forward to your first lesson," she said.

And amazingly, so did he.

"You have got to be kidding me."

Elizabeth stared at the fire-engine red Corvette convertible sitting in the Magnolia Cove Fire Department parking lot, then at the keys in her hand. She and Sully had walked there after breakfast, to pick up his car.

And what a car it turned out to be.

"What's wrong?" Sully asked, glancing from her to the line of grinning men behind them.

"You expect to learn to drive again in *that?*" she asked incredulously.

Sully looked confused. "Is there a problem?"

She muttered an oath under her breath regarding the vanity of the male species, then plastered a smile on her face. "Okay, then. Hop in."

With a nod, he headed for the passenger seat.

"Whoa, there! Aren't you driving?"

"I'd prefer not to. If you don't mind."

She balked. She drove a Prius. Economical. Responsible. Reliable. But she knew all about men and their machines. Obsessive. A fire chief and his red 'Vette had to be among the worst. "Sully, have you ever let anyone else on the planet even sit in the driver's seat?"

"I, um…"

She checked with the half-dozen firefighters watching them from the sidelines. To a man—including the one woman—they all shook their heads, grins firmly in place.

"Hey, if you don't feel like driving the 'Vette anymore," one of the firemen called. "I'll trade you for my Chevy!"

The others laughed. "Yeah," another said, "or my old truck."

To her surprise, Sully called back, "I might take you up on that, Jeremy Swift!" as they awkwardly slid into the low-slung sports car. "What color is it?"

"Blue," the man yelled as she turned the key and brought the engine to life with a roar. "What's left of the paint."

Sully waved to the guys, and she could swear his teeth were clenched. "Always hated red," he muttered through them.

Nervously she let the clutch out. The 'Vette leaped from the parking lot onto the main street. Sully's eyes were squeezed shut.

Despite herself, she laughed. "Come on, I'm not that bad a driver," she said.

He cracked them open and peered at her. "Sorry. Don't really care for— *God's Bones!*" She had stopped at a light and he was staring at a road sign behind her. "*Fouquet Street?* They named a blasted street after—"

His words halted abruptly as his gaze collided with hers. He smiled self-consciously.

"Tricks again?" she asked, smiling back.

That cute chagrin swept over his face. "Lizzie—"

"It's okay. I don't mind you being a pirate. It can be our little secret." Hell, she didn't even mind him calling her Lizzie, a name she'd always disliked.

He studied her with his dark, bedroom eyes, his beautiful lips turned down at the corners. "You must think me a raving lunatic."

Frankly it was probably *her* who was the lunatic. Because suddenly all she could think about was kissing those lips again.

"Heavens, no," she said, and turned resolutely forward. The light blinked green and the car jumped to life. "Which way?" she asked. The welcome home party was at the number one station house of the Old Fort Mystic Fire Department, on the mainland, where Sully was chief, not the tiny local and mostly volunteer fire station where the car had been parked.

"No clue. I was hoping you knew."

She chuckled. "We could go back and ask."

He looked pained.

"Or not. Maybe there's a map in the glove compartment."

He blinked.

Wow. The man wasn't kidding. He really did have amnesia.

Briefly she wondered how he'd remembered how to kiss so well. She glanced at him and smiled. Some things must come naturally.

She pointed at the glove compartment and guided him to the correct map, coaching him how to unfold and read it.

Luckily he was a fast learner.

But she wasn't going to think about *that*.

"Chief!"

As soon as they arrived at the Old Fort Mystic FD, the men and women all descended on Sully, gingerly slapping his back, giving him hugs, punching him lightly in the arm in a ritual of genuine happiness over his recovery and return. Elizabeth was touched by how much everyone had missed their chief and how glad they were to have him back.

In Sully's honor they had prepared a sumptuous barbecue, complete with chicken, corn on the cob, grill-baked potatoes and a multitude of salads brought in by spouses, who were also in attendance.

No one was particularly surprised that he had Elizabeth in tow. She felt a little out of place as she ate and talked and wandered around with him, especially given the looks she was getting from the men—as though one and all assumed they were sleeping together, and not one was surprised or asked about Lisa Grosvenor. Good grief. If driving a Corvette weren't a big enough clue, this clinched it. Andre Sullivan was a certified lady's man.

She didn't know why that bothered her so much. After all, she was just here for a few days and had no intention of even kissing him again, let alone sleeping with the man. She wanted only one thing from Sully—a blood test for bone marrow compatibility with Caleb. Nothing more.

There was no logical reason for the pique she was feeling. What he did with other women was absolutely none of her business. He certainly wouldn't be doing it with *her.*

When he walked up and put his hand on her shoulder and asked, "Lizzie, would you like—" She shot to her feet.

"No!" she snapped. "And don't call me Lizzie!"

At his look of surprised rebuff, she shut her eyes and counted to ten. When she opened them again, she gave him an apologetic look. "I'm sorry. That was rude of me. Blame it on PMS."

He raised his brow uncomprehendingly. "PM…?"

She wasn't about to go *there.* "Never mind. I was thinking I should probably—"

"How about a drive?"

Surprised, she asked, "You're ready to go home so soon?"

They'd been at the station nearly two hours, but she'd gotten the impression that other than being called to a fire, the guys who worked here weren't in a hurry about much of anything.

"*Non.* To a friend's house. There's someone I need to talk to."

After saying their goodbyes, he settled into the 'Vette with a long sigh.

"What?" she asked, turning the car back toward Frenchman's Island.

"I feel like such a fraud," he said. "I don't remember any of them. Or my job. Or…"

She glanced over sympathetically as he fell silent.

What must that be like? Not to remember anything about one's life. Not that she personally would miss all that much about her own—other than her family and the few friends she still had. After high school most of them had gone off to college and not returned to their small village. But she had stayed behind to help Don and Gilda with the farm. The Sullivan estate was large and they were getting older. Until Caleb grew up—

She banished her thoughts about herself and determinedly returned them to Sully. Regardless of the emptiness of one's life it would be awful not to remember any of it.

"It'll all come back to you," she said. "I'm sure it will."

He rolled his head on the seat back and gave her a dry smile, but didn't comment. "Have you ever been sailing?" he asked a few minutes later.

"A time or two." Growing up close to the Connecticut coast, she'd spent most summers on the deck of the family cabin cruiser. But several of her childhood friends had owned sailboats.

"We should go sailing. I haven't been in…ages."

"You own a Corvette *and* a boat? Not bad, Sullivan."

"Actually I don't. But my friend does. We can borrow his."

She wasn't sure how she felt about being stuck with Sully on a tiny vessel, wearing a tiny bathing suit and being surrounded by nothing but ocean. Probably not a great idea. So it was particularly maddening when she found herself saying, "That sounds fun."

"Good. I'll ask Mrs. Yates when we get there. Turn here," he said, pointing out a narrow oyster shell path leading into the dense junglelike forest. The vegetation on Frenchman's Island was lush, green and wild. Palmettos mingled with giant oaks and other hardwoods, thick bushes and flowering vines. Waist-high grasses grew near the meandering shoreline and down into the water.

"Who's Mrs. Yates?"

"My friend Tyree's housekeeper. He and his new wife are off on their honeymoon. Mrs. Yates is taking care of Rose Cottage while they're gone."

In Elizabeth's eyes, Rose Cottage was more like Rose Manor.

"Wow, it's beautiful," she said as she climbed out.

The three-story historic mansion had flowing lines with an abundance of floor-to ceiling bays and mullioned windows, sweeping porches and grand galleries. A widow's walk skimmed along the roofline overlooking the inlet behind the house. There was even a small mother-in-law cottage out back, surrounded by an overflowing English garden.

"Give us a hand, *chère,*" Sully said. He was still in the 'Vette, struggling to stand.

She hurried around the car to help him. He was tall, very tall, and it was a long way up from the bucket seat. She took his hands and tugged, eventually getting him up, but sending him right into her arms.

He didn't seem to object. His arms came around her and he drew her close.

Her pulse kicked up. "Sully," she whispered, loathe to pull away but knowing she had no business staying in his embrace. He felt so good. So hard and lean and strong.

But so wrong.

She took a deep breath and tried to step back. But he wouldn't let go.

"What's his name?" he asked, his voice low and gravelly.

"Who?"

"Your man."

Her heart beat faster. "I don't have a man," she admitted. "No boyfriend."

She'd always been too busy with school, the farm and her job for more than casual dates. And then when Caleb got sick, there was no time for men. Every spare minute she had she'd spent with her brother.

Caleb.

Sully leaned back and looked into her eyes. "But last night, you said…"

She swallowed. *This was her chance.* "There is someone I want to tell you about. But it's not a man. He's my brother."

"Your—" Sully's eyes widened, and his mouth curved into a dazzling smile. "*Mon Dieu,* Lizzie! Here I thought…" He pulled her tight to his chest. "Thank God."

"Sully, listen. There's something I need to—"

But suddenly, the front door of Rose Cottage opened wide and a plump, gray-haired lady scooted out onto the porch.

"As I live and breathe!" she declared with a cheerful laugh. "Why, it's none other than Captain Sullivan Fouquet!"

Chapter 3

The look on Elizabeth's face was priceless.

Sully grinned at old Mrs. Yates. Having worked as Tyree's caretaker going on twenty years now—nearly all while he was still a ghost—she knew exactly what was going on. And exactly who Sully was. She'd even met Andre Sullivan a few days before he died, and was in fact present at the fiery accident where Sully's spirit had somehow reanimated Andre's lifeless body.

Mrs. Yates had long ago accepted that the impossible was possible. Sully, a bit more recently.

Elizabeth was obviously still working on the concept.

At her look, Mrs. Yates gave another laugh and said, "Dear me, did I say Captain Fouquet? Naturally I meant Chief Sullivan. Come in, come in! I'll put on some tea."

Once inside, Sully introduced Elizabeth. At her

name, Mrs. Yates's eyebrows rose and she shot him a quick glance. She knew the details of his past life, including his fiancée, Elizabeth Hayden, the accidental shooting of whom had led to his and Tyree's infamous fatal duel two hundred years ago.

"Elizabeth *Hamilton,*" he emphasized, shaking his head almost imperceptibly.

But Elizabeth didn't catch the exchange because she was too busy staring at a large painting that graced the center hallway. A painting of himself and Tyree in the prime of their privateering days. One of their friend Thom Bowden's overly melodramatic works done in oils, it showed them on the deck of the *Sea Nymph,* armed to the teeth, ready to take an enemy vessel by force. Thom Bowden never had a coin to his name, but had been a likable enough fellow, always hanging out at the Moon and Palmetto sketching portraits for ale and grocery money. He, Tyree and their ships were frequently the subjects of his paintings.

And the uncanny likeness of his old self to Andre was unmistakable in this one.

"Good grief," she murmured. "No wonder you identified with the man. You're a dead ringer."

He hid a wince. "Aye. You might say that."

"Was he some kind of distant relative?"

He cleared his throat. "In a manner of speaking."

"Who's the other guy?"

"His partner, Captain Tyree St. James."

Her dubious gaze turned to his. "Tyree?"

He cleared his throat again. "*Alors.* My friend on his honeymoon, his name is really James Tyler. I just call him…" He realized he was only digging himself deeper and glanced around for a distraction. Suddenly his whole body froze in shock. There, mounted on the wall above the fireplace in a salon just off the hall was a pair of crossed sabers.

His saber. And Tyree's. The very swords they'd dueled with two hundred years earlier. The swords with which they'd killed one another.

Sacre coeur. He took a deep breath and shook off the eerie feeling, tearing his gaze from the instruments of his own destruction.

Elizabeth looked from the painting to him, to the sabers and back, questions clearly shining in her eyes.

He shrugged, and gave her an awkward grin. "Sorry. What was I saying?"

Luckily Mrs. Yates came to his rescue. "Never mind. Kitchen's this way," she said, herding them away from the painting and the swords, toward the back of the house. "I'll put on a kettle and tell you the news from Captain St…. Captain James, shall I?"

He dragged himself back to the present.

"James was—is—my best friend, who has been a constant presence at the hospital during my recovery. He and his wife, Clara, are on a year-long sail around the world," he explained to Elizabeth, shifting his concentration to her long, sexy legs as he followed behind, amazed as he had been last night, at the amount of skin she was showing. He was still getting used to the revealing clothing women wore these days. Not that he was complaining about her short skirt, mind you. "Clara is a travel writer."

"And James?" she asked as they took seats around a

giant antique clawfoot table and Mrs. Yates fussed with tea things.

"James is…an eccentric," Sully said with a chuckle. "He likes to sail and to collect old things." He peeled his gaze from Elizabeth's mouthwateringly sexy T-shirt and looked around the kitchen counters, which were crammed full of a multitude of shiny electrical gadgets and cooking implements. "*And* new things. He's a bit of a fool for those…what are they called? Online auctions?"

Mrs. Yates rolled her eyes. "Much to the joy of the local women's shelters. It's a pain to keep up with him, but he's very generous. Next, though, I expect it'll be baby things."

Sully jerked up in his seat. "Baby things?"

She cackled happily. "A pretty new wife, a whole year in a tiny sailboat cabin and no TV? You do the math, Captain."

The thought of Tyree having a child was too bizarre. He'd always been the confirmed bachelor with a woman in every port. Sully was the one who'd longed for wife and family. He glanced at Elizabeth. She hadn't wanted children before. Would this new Elizabeth want them? He hoped so.

"How romantic would that be?" she murmured with a wistful smile. Perhaps she did…

His heart squeezed with the distant but familiar pang of his love for her, filling with memories of the blissful days and nights they'd spent together so long ago. She'd been a wonderful companion. Spontaneous and full of laughter, always ready with open arms when he came home from a voyage. Her disposition was cheerful, her nature passionate.

He wanted those days back. And even more, the nights.

Mrs. Yates had been chatting on about e-mails she'd received from Clara and Tyree, and brought him back to the present by addressing him. "They send greetings, Captain, and a reminder to set up the laptop computer Captain James gave you."

He grimaced. Tyree was wild for all the newfangled stuff his friend called "technology." With Tyree, it was online this and online that. Rose Cottage was now practically a fortress with all the electronic security measures Tyree installed before consenting to leave Mrs. Yates by herself for a year. Which was a good thing because Sully would have been useless as a guard in his present condition. But as for technology, hell, Sully was still getting used to zippers on his pants instead of buttons. He wondered if Elizabeth's skirt had a zipper....

She smiled over at him. "I'll help you get it up and running, if you want."

He was thinking more of getting it *down,* and her not running.

Her eyebrow raised.

Ah. The laptop. He returned her smile wryly. It was a humbling experience having a woman know more than he about pretty much everything around him. "I'll have to start paying you as my secretary," he muttered. "Or my nursemaid."

"Don't be ridiculous. I'm happy to help," she said.

For which he was very grateful. Especially if she continued to wear that skirt.

But for a split second he wondered why she offered him so much of her time.

Dismissing the thought, when Mrs. Yates served the tea, he took the opportunity to broach the subject he really wanted to talk about. "I spoke with Jake Santee today."

She handed him his cup. "The arson investigator at Old Fort Mystic?"

He took a deep breath of the fragrant orange spice tea, the scent exploding over his newly liberated senses. "He moved his office here to the Magnolia Cove station part-time. And he's closed the case."

He didn't need to say which one.

"But they never found Peel!" she objected, setting the pot down with a clatter. "Or his body."

Wesley Peel was the prime suspect in a string of arson cases over the past year, culminating in the fire at the historic pub in which the arsonist supposedly died.

Only Sully, Tyree, his wife Clara and Mrs. Yates knew about the more incredible, otherworldly results of that fire—Sully's transmigration and the lifting of the curse that had held Tyree prisoner as a wandering spirit for two centuries—that had caused both men to become mortal again.

The thought that a witness to those events might be lurking about somewhere, with nefarious purpose and uncertain means, made Sully uneasy. Not to mention Tyree's suspicions…

"Jake said he was getting pressure from the mayor," Sully said, savoring the tang of the citrus tea as it slid over his tongue. "He was not happy to close it, but had no evidence Wesley Peel *wasn't* dead."

"True, there have been no more fires since."

"How many fires did this man set?" Elizabeth asked.

"Five," he said. "All very old buildings on the historical register."

"Strange choice for an arsonist."

"The theory was, he was searching for something specific. And when he didn't find it, he burned the places down."

"What was he looking for?" she asked, openly curious.

"He always took paintings," Mrs. Yates supplied, "by a certain artist, Thom Bowden—the man who painted the one in the hall you were admiring. And also volumes from a set of old journals. Peel appeared to be after one diary in particular."

"A diary?" Elizabeth asked incredulously.

Mrs. Yates poured her another cup of tea. "Yes. Written by one of the sailors on the *Sea Sprite,* sister ship to Sullivan Fouquet's *Sea Nymph.*"

"Ah." Her eyes brightened in understanding. "A pirate treasure map!"

"Wesley Peel's ancestor, John Peel, was said to have discovered one of Fouquet and St. James's buried treasure chests after their deaths, and built the Peel family fortune upon it. A lumber mill," Sully supplied. Tyree had uncovered that information in his research. "The mill recently went bankrupt. It's possible Wesley Peel thought there was more treasure to be found somewhere, and he could save his family's business."

Of course, there isn't. Tyree had recovered the remaining chests nearly two hundred years ago, founding his own fortune. Recently he'd given much of his wealth away, but enough remained to keep them all comfortable for life, including Sully, to whom Tyree had insisted on signing over half before leaving on his honeymoon.

Mrs. Yates gave Sully a surreptitious glance. "Captain James thinks it more likely Peel is after the words to a potent voudou curse."

Elizabeth's jaw dropped. "Voudou? In a *pirate diary?*"

"Privateer," Sully swiftly corrected, stepping in to steer the conversation away from that particular patch of quicksand. He couldn't believe Mrs. Yates had mentioned it.

Elizabeth blinked. "Right. Privateer. I read something about that. What exactly is the difference?"

"A pirate is an outlaw," he explained. "A privateer has letters of marque from his government, authorizing him to seize enemy ships on their behalf. All legal and aboveboard."

When Sully had first been forcibly transported to South Louisiana from Lord Henry Sullivan's estate in Connecticut, in youthful bitterness he'd signed on with one of the notorious pirate ships that plied their trade around the gulf and Caribbean. He'd done well. Very well. But when the War of Independence came along, he'd jumped at the chance to sail for the newly formed revolutionary government. As a side-benefit he'd received a full pardon for all previous crimes. Then he'd met Tyree, and the rest, as they say, was history. Literally.

"Okay," she said. "But what made this Peel guy think a privateering diary contained a voudou curse, of all things?"

He should have known she wouldn't be distracted.

He puffed out a breath. Mrs. Yates rose to fetch a

plate of her home-baked macaroons from the pantry. Somewhere in another room a mantel clock chimed twice. And Sully decided since they'd gone this far, he might as well tell the whole truth.

"A well-known legend has it that a powerful Haitian voudou priest, Jeantout, taught Sullivan Fouquet his secrets in exchange for saving his life. Fouquet's dying words were said to have been a two-hundred-year-long curse on the man who'd accidentally killed his fiancée."

"Tyree St. James," Elizabeth murmured.

"Aye," Sully said, suppressing a shudder at the sharp memory of cold steel slicing through his gullet and rage over Elizabeth's death. "Supposedly this voudou curse was written down word for word in the journal of an eyewitness, Davey Scraggs."

"The sailor from the *Sea Sprite.*"

"Aye." *The old busybody.* Everything that ever happened to any man on either crew was dutifully scribbled down in those blasted journals. Scraggs could have been rich through blackmail alone if he hadn't had the integrity of a parson. Sully hadn't been a bit surprised when Tyree had told him Scraggs continued to write journals until his death, many years after Sully's own.

She raised a skeptical brow. "So, Peel thought if he read or spoke the words of this voudou curse, what would happen?"

Sully grimaced and turned his attention to more pleasant fare—the plate of macaroons. "Who knows. The man lost the family business and all his money. Maybe he believed if he didn't find the treasure, voudou could get it all back for him."

"Was that the arson investigator's theory?"

Sully bit into one of the sweet cakes with an appreciative hum. "To be sure, Jake Santee didn't so much care *why* Peel was setting fires," he hedged. "Only that he *was* setting fires."

For a long moment he could feel her eyes on him. Weighing. "But you care," she finally said. "Why?"

Merde. Leave it to her to get right at the heart of the matter.

He set down the macaroon. "Because Wesley Peel is a madman," he answered. That much, at least, was true. "And because he tried to kill my best friends. Mrs. Yates herself barely escaped the fire unscathed." Also true. "And because I believe Peel is still alive. And that he'll stop at nothing to get what he is after." And that was what really worried him.

He met her gaze, and saw the color drain from her face as she realized the meaning beneath his words.

Her voice was unsteady as she said, "And since it was in all the newspapers how you awoke from your coma thinking you were Sullivan Fouquet…" she whispered, "this time, he'll be coming after *you.*"

Suddenly the amusing quirkiness of Sully's trick memory took on a whole different quality. Frightening. Dangerous. Anything but amusing.

"Oh, my God," Elizabeth said, aghast. "What are you going to do?"

"Not much I can do," he answered all too calmly. "Not until Peel shows himself."

"What about the journal? Where is that?"

"With Peel," Sully said. "Wherever that might be."

"He got all of them," Mrs. Yates explained. "Stolen from the houses before he set them ablaze."

"Including the volume with the curse?"

"Aye. It had been in Clara James's possession. But he was able to steal it from her."

At that, Elizabeth's anxiety notched down a bit. "Then he's read it. And surely must realize by now that the curse is just nonsense. That it doesn't work."

Sully and the old woman shifted in their seats.

After a moment of hushed discomfort, Sully said, "I must compliment you on your excellent macaroons, Mrs. Yates. They are truly delicious."

"Why, thank you, Captain," she chimed in. "I have some oatmeal-raisin, too, if you'd care to try those?"

He grinned wolfishly. "You should know better than to tempt a man like that. I'll certainly not refuse."

Elizabeth watched the exchange with stark disbelief. She wasn't sure what perplexed her more, Sully's almost orgasmic enjoyment of his simple tea and cookies, Mrs. Yates consistently calling him "Captain" rather than "Chief," or their almost conspiratorial silence—and therefore tacit disagreement—regarding her observation about the curse.

"Oatmeal-raisin, dear?" Mrs. Yates asked, extending the plate toward her.

Elizabeth stood abruptly. "What on earth are you two playing at?"

They both blinked at her innocently. "Whatever can you mean, my dear?"

Good grief. She spun to Sully. "Please don't tell me

you buy into this curse thing. Lord, Sully, tell me you don't somehow still think you really are a two-hundred-year-old pirate!"

He actually squirmed. "*Chère,* I know this will probably be difficult to believe, but—"

She slapped her hands over her ears. "Andre Sullivan, I do *not* want to hear this!"

Unfortunately, she was pretty good at reading lips. The swearword he muttered as he rose and reached for her was fairly clear.

He grasped her wrists and pulled her hands away from her ears. "Lizzie, none of that matters. It's what's inside a man that counts, *non?*"

She wanted to agree. Really, she did. And she hoped like hell he meant it. For Caleb's sake. But for hers…her heart couldn't help but sink.

Not that it should matter one iota if the man was crazy as a loon. She had no personal stake in his sanity or insanity. None at all. But still…

"Yes, you're right," she said, trying desperately to be reasonable. "I just worry, that's all."

He looked absurdly pleased. "About me?"

She wanted to groan. "Andre—"

"*Sully.*"

She huffed impatiently. "The point is, if Wesley Peel really is still alive, and you persist in this…insane delusion…it could get you killed!"

"I've faced scarier men than Peel in my day," he assured her with a kiss on her forehead.

Why did that so not comfort her?

She looked to the older woman for help, but Mrs. Yates

just beamed at the tender way Sully took Elizabeth into his arms. There would be no support from *that* quarter.

Elizabeth sighed, and for a brief moment let herself enjoy the warm contact with the infuriating man's tall, strong body. Though she'd known him less than a day, and he was being remarkably presumptuous, it felt exactly right to be in his embrace, pressed close to his muscular chest, her cheek resting on his broad shoulder. She had an almost irresistible urge to lift her face and let his lips meet hers. As they had in the garden yesterday. As she'd so desperately wanted to last night when he was in her bed.

Damn.

She really had to tell him why she was here in Magnolia Cove. Soon.

Pulling away, she avoided his gaze, but he snagged her hand so she couldn't escape completely.

"Mrs. Yates," he said, ignoring her not-so-subtle tugs, "before he sailed, Tyree said he'd leave a package with you for me?"

"Oh, yes. I'd completely forgotten about that. I'll run and fetch it for you."

She bustled out of the kitchen, and Elizabeth was left alone with Sully, still trying to extract her hand from his.

"It's no use, you know," he said, turning to her.

"What is?"

"Denying your attraction to me."

She gave one last yank. "Who's denying it?"

A second later she landed back in his arms again with an *oof.* "You're not?"

"I think it's been pretty obvious I find you quite, um—" *sexy, desirable, appealing* "—attractive."

Far too attractive for her own good.

His smile blazed back at her. "I'm glad to hear it. I was afraid you were avoiding touching me."

With that, his mouth came down on hers. She wasn't exactly surprised, but gave a small gasp nonetheless. Which let him in—to her consternation...and her pleasure.

She moaned softly. Balanced on the brink. But his tongue swept into her mouth, bringing with it the taste of sweet macaroons and male desire. An irresistible combination. She wrapped her arms around his neck and returned the kiss. And for a short, blissful minute forgot about everything but the exquisite sensation of falling for—

Oh, no! She jerked back, suddenly coming to her senses.

"I *am* avoiding you," she said contritely, sliding from his embrace. "I keep telling you, there's—"

"Here it is!" Mrs. Yates sang out cheerily. She walked into the kitchen carrying a large black folio, which looked like the ones artists used to carry their loose drawings or paintings.

Sully looked irritated for a second, but he quickly masked it and accepted the portfolio from Mrs. Yates. "What's in here?"

"Captain James's notes on Wesley Peel and the fires, I believe. A few other odds and ends. A drawing he recovered from your old town house. Oh, and the key."

His eyes widened in surprise. "Key?"

"To your old place. Unfortunately you can't live there. It's slated for demolition. The captain was able to stall the Magnolia Cove planning commission, but he's unsure how long they'll put off tearing it down. The building became unsafe during the last hurricane."

Elizabeth got the distinct feeling he wanted to ask more, but he just nodded, tucked the folio under his arm, thanked Mrs. Yates for it and her hospitality and herded Elizabeth out the front door to his car.

"Back to the Pirate's Rest?" she asked nervously, getting behind the wheel. Still thinking about their kiss.

But his face held a strange, faraway expression. "*Non.* I want to go by my old town house."

It seemed there was something else on his mind. Relief mingled with an irrational spike of disappointment. "Is it here on the island? The town house."

He nodded. "In the village, just a few blocks from where the fire was."

"Where you were injured, you mean?"

"I'd like to see that, too."

"Are you sure?"

His eyes met hers and he smiled, but he seemed preoccupied. "You needn't worry, I'll be fine. Simply curious."

She shouldn't be surprised he'd so quickly dismissed their kiss. She knew his reputation. It would take far more than a mere kiss to be memorable to a lady's man like him.

Which was a good thing, she reminded herself. Because she wasn't here for kisses.

The village of Magnolia Cove was only a mile or two down the main road, a quaint, sleepy place that looked like it was stuck in a time warp. Which was the main appeal. Tourists came here looking for antiques, centuries-old architecture and charming old restaurants and pubs. And the Pirate Museum and Pirate Festival, of course. The place was certifiably pirate crazy.

Thank goodness she'd missed the festival, held in August, and she had no intention of visiting the museum. She'd never had the slightest interest in pirates.

Well. Until very recently.

And now only as the subject of oblique irritation and unease.

She followed his directions once they got to the village, and pulled up in front of a truly ancient block of row houses.

"When were these built?" she asked, amazed the narrow two-story timbered town houses were still standing. Part of the roof had blown off one end, and all four attached houses were leaning observably to the left. No wonder the city council had condemned them. A large yellow sign was attached to each of its four doors, warning no admittance by order of the Fire Department.

He winked. "That would be me," he said. With a flourish he produced the key he'd fished out of the portfolio earlier and approached the first door on the right. "Now, I understand if you don't want to come in with me. I'm just going to take a quick look."

She debated for a second, then followed him inside. If they'd stood for this long, they'd probably last another ten minutes.

She trailed behind as he meandered through the dark rooms of the ground floor, dank with disuse and dusty with neglect. It wasn't a large place, but it had once been beautiful. The wood appointments were elegant, the cracked plaster relief work on the ceiling had once been intricate and graceful. There were a few tall windows, caked with grime.

"Can't see much," she ventured, staying close behind him. She could imagine that all sorts of creatures had taken up residence in place of the humans. "When did you live here?"

He paused in front of the staircase and glanced up it. "A long time ago," he murmured. "Want to go upstairs?"

She was just opening her mouth to say no way in hell when he grabbed the banister and started up the staircase leaning heavily on his cane as he ascended.

"Okay, sure," she said, suddenly not wanting to be left behind. For some reason, the place was starting to give her the creeps. Almost like it was...watching her.

"Where are you going?" she asked, hurrying after.

"Bedroom," he said, heading toward a door at the end of the short hallway. "There's something I need to get."

"Get?" She grasped the door frame and peered inside the room, adjusting her eyes to the even dimmer light.

"I left something here. I want to retrieve it."

With a frown, he opened another door, to what looked like a closet. "This is new," he mused.

"Sully, you can't just come in here and take things. The building belongs to—"

"Tyree. That is, James Tyler. He mentioned it while I was in the hospital." He disappeared into the closet.

Nervously she went into the room and walked over to it. "Sully?"

She could hear him muttering and fumbling around, but it was totally dark inside so she couldn't see a thing.

Suddenly she heard a crash and wood splintering. Along with a string of French-sounding words she was glad she didn't know what meant.

"Sully!"

"Damned paneling. I— Ah, here it is." A moment later there was another string of French words. "It's empty." He sounded grim.

"What is?"

"My hidey-hole. I was hoping…" He appeared at the door, shaking his head. "Never mind. There's one other place I need to check."

He went from that bedroom to another, which was situated at the short end of the building and therefore had more windows and was a little brighter. Striding directly to the brick fireplace on the outer wall, he ran his fingertips gingerly along the underside of the mantel. Setting aside his cane, he knelt down awkwardly, grasped a section of the brick flanking the fireplace and with a grunt slid it aside, revealing a cavity of about a foot square. Inside the opening lay several dark brown bags.

He turned to look up at her, his expression triumphant. "He didn't know about these."

"Who?"

"Tyree."

"James Tyler? You believe he took whatever was in the other hidey-hole?"

"Almost certainly. He might have said, but much of what he told me early on in the hospital is a blur… Anyway, he'll be surprised to see these."

She watched as he pulled one of the bags out, wondering at the nature of Sully and James Tyler's relationship. Sully claimed they were best friends, but there seemed to be some kind of tension there. As evidenced by this little secret.

"Here, help me put them up on the mantel," he directed as he handed her the first bag, and began pulling the others from their hiding place.

"Oh, my God," she exclaimed when the weight of it nearly dragged her hands to the floor as she accepted it. She barely managed to hoist the bag up onto the mantelpiece. "What the hell do you have in here, anyway? Gold bricks?"

She braced herself for the second bag.

"Mais, non," he said with a chuckle. "Not bricks, *chère.* They would never fit in these small bags. It's coins," he said, handing it up to her. "Gold coins."

Chapter 4

Sully was ready to grab the leather bag as it fell from Elizabeth's hand.

"Gold c-coins?" she sputtered.

He'd had a feeling that would be her reaction. Women were so easily impressed. He handed the bag back and indicated the mantel. He dare not leave them hidden here lest they be destroyed along with the building, and he needed help carrying them. But how to explain…?

"Spanish doubloons, I believe. From…Sullivan Fouquet's last voyage."

"And how did you come by them?" she asked, wide-eyed.

She was not going to like the explanation that they were his secret stash from a previous lifetime.

He cleared his throat and passed her the third heavy bag. "Honestly, I assure you."

Alors, as honestly as capturing an enemy merchant-man could be considered. It had been an incredible boarding. Not a shot had been fired, but the prize had been fat. The Spanish ship was heavy with cargo just taken onboard in Hispaniola, gathered from the far reaches of South America and the Caribbean. Rum, emeralds, cotton, sugar, silver and a strong box filled with gold coins collected as taxes from the wealthy colonial plantation owners. What a catch!

He glanced up and realized Elizabeth was staring at him. "What?"

"You're grinning like a pirate." Her dry tone held a slight note of accusation.

He laughed and held out the last bag for her. "Remembering good times," he said, and rose to his feet, shaking out the stiffness in his knee.

On impulse, he reached out and grasped her behind the neck, pulling her to him for a quick kiss. He couldn't get enough of her mouth, which was somehow softer, more pliable than it had been two centuries ago. He wanted to spend the entire day kissing her, getting to know her lovely mouth again.

Except, there was still a slight hesitation in her acceptance of his lips on hers.

He hadn't quite won her over yet. He would have to work on that.

"Can you carry one of the bags down the stairs?" he asked, letting her go before she could pull away herself. She nodded, and he gathered the three remaining leather bags to his chest, grabbed his cane and followed.

When they were seated in the car, the gold safely tucked on the floor by his boots, she turned in her seat and gazed at him for several moments.

"Are you going to tell me what's really going on?" she asked.

He frowned. "I'm not sure what you mean."

"You claim to have amnesia, yet just now you said you were remembering good times. You claim there is no treasure map in those journals, that the arsonist Wesley Peel is after some crazy voudou thing, and yet, lo and behold, you just happen to be in possession of a priceless pirate treasure."

Ah. So not the kisses. "Elizabeth…"

"Care to explain all that?"

He closed his eyes and let the battle play out in his mind. He hated deception more than anything. He had a volatile enough nature without throwing lies into the mix. Though, admittedly, because of his past profession he'd occasionally been forced to speak false.

But in this case the truth of his knowledge was so fantastical, she would sooner believe a fiction. And yet it rankled.

He did not *want* to be Andre Sullivan.

"Perhaps," he finally said, "it's best you do not ask."

Her pretty mouth, still pink from his kisses, thinned. "Very well."

She drove in silence to the Pirate's Rest Inn and wordlessly made two trips up the stairs to his room when his leg couldn't manage the steps and the heavy burden of three bags at one time.

"Elizabeth," he said when she turned to go, desperate to make her understand. Somehow. He reached for her. "Please believe me. It's not what you are thinking."

Her back bristled and she stepped back. "How could you possibly know what I'm thinking?" she quietly demanded.

"Because I know what *I'd* be thinking," he returned.

His guarded distrust had saved his life on many an occasion. But it had also been troublesome at times. Hadn't he even begun to suspect that Elizabeth Hayden was secretly seeing someone else those last months they were together? Hadn't he been dead certain it was Tyree? A foolish notion his friend had set to rights immediately upon Sully's waking in the hospital. Seeing Tyree with his Clara was proof enough of the matter. Those stars in his eyes had not been there when he'd looked upon any woman in the past, certainly not Elizabeth Hayden.

He didn't want this new Elizabeth to distrust him. Not for anything.

"I'll get your folio," she said shortly, and whisked out of his room.

He wanted to stop her, to compel her to stay with him and let him explain. But he thought better of it. He would like to see the notes Tyree had left for him in the folio, and knew he'd never make it down and up three flights again without resting his leg first.

He cursed his infirmity, and hated the discord that had sprung up between him and Elizabeth. How could he make it right again without lies? And without tying her to his bed and convincing her with his body…

When she returned and handed him the folio, he took it with one hand and grasped her fingers with the other.

"Will you stay and help me with the laptop?" he asked.

She bit her lip. "I don't think—"

"Please?"

After a slight hesitation, she said, "All right. But after dinner," she said. "I need to talk with you about something anyway."

"About what?"

She shook her head, as she checked her wristwatch. "Later. I promised to call my mother before dinner." With that, she pulled her hand free and hurried out the door, closing it softly behind her.

Alors. At least she was still speaking to him.

He needed a distraction, so he wouldn't go after her. Crawl down the damn stairs if he had to.

With a sigh he removed his boots and hoisted himself onto the high, four-poster bed, leaning against the solid walnut headboard while stretching his legs out on the fancy lace coverlet. Reaching for the portfolio, he untied the strings holding the top together and emptied the contents onto the bed.

A sheaf of handwritten papers fluttered down onto a much larger piece of cardboard. He flipped through the papers, immediately recognizing Tyree's slanted scrawl.

As promised, there were notes on each of the fires set by Wesley Peel, along with a couple of pages dealing with Peel himself—his background, family history and the sawmill business he'd recently lost. There was also a page in a different hand, listing what appeared to be various theories on Peel's motivation for his crimes. Several of them had been crossed out. Curiosity compelled him to read those which remained.

2) voudou curse (explains diaries but not paintings)
4) obsession with Sullivan Fouquet/pirates
5) believes there's more treasure
8) something we don't know about
9) he's just crazy and there's no connection to anything

He chuckled at the last one, imagining Clara's exasperated face as she wrote it.

Setting the papers aside, he picked up the thick piece of cardboard. It measured about three feet wide by two feet tall. Upon closer examination he realized it was really two pieces tied together with string, sandwiching something between. He snapped the string and the top layer of cardboard fell away, revealing—

The breath caught in his lungs as he immediately recognized what lay under.

Evidence of treachery!

He'd forgotten about Thom Bowden's unfinished canvas. Sully had discovered it hidden among Elizabeth Hayden's things on the day before he died, but never had the opportunity to ask her about the drawing—which illustrated the secret location where he and Tyree had buried the lion's share of their privateering profits.

Back then, Sully had immediately suspected Elizabeth and Tyree had become sexually involved and were plotting against him. It was one reason he'd been so quick to the sword the night of their duel. But recent conversations in the hospital had proven to Sully without a shadow of a doubt that Tyree had not betrayed him with Elizabeth.

Sully studied Thom's faded pencil drawings on the brittle canvas. He would recognize the configuration of the small islands anywhere.

So how had the drawing ended up concealed amongst the folded bits of her clothing? One thing was certain, she could not have plotted alone. Elizabeth was many things, but overly clever was not one of them. If not with Tyree, then whom?

Had she conspired with Thom Bowden, the artist? Had she followed Tyree and Sully to the hidden cache, then brought Thom Bowden back to paint the location? Tyree's notes said Thom died years later in his perpetual state of finances—poor as a ship's rat. The treasure island had certainly been drawn by him, but he must not have had any idea of the riches that lay hidden on its shores while doing so.

Tyree's notes also claimed there was a passage in one of the journals where Davey Scraggs told of a sailor called John Peel who got drunk and bragged that he'd covertly followed the captains one night, and soon he'd be a rich man. If that was true, it was probably John Peel who'd commissioned the drawing from Thom Bowden, taking him out to paint the island, lest he forget its location.

But then how had Elizabeth come by it? John Peel was an older man with a passel of kids, a homely man who loved his wife and enjoyed his family life. Sully couldn't see Elizabeth Hayden becoming involved with a man like that. Not even for a chest full of gold and jewels.

And yet, according to Tyree's notes, John Peel did indeed find the treasure. But he only took one single chest of the many hidden there, and not until five whole years after Sully and Tyree's fatal duel. Why had Peel not returned for the treasure sooner? Especially since Sully and Tyree were conveniently dead and wouldn't be around to object?

Sully did not care for the most likely reason—that the person who had possession of the map to the treasure had died around the same time they did.

Because there really was only one person who fit that description on both counts. Their betrayer surely was none other than his dear fiancée, Elizabeth.

Dinner was a bit tense.

Elizabeth was glad for Mrs. Butterfield's steady monologue of village gossip, spiced with suggestions as to how her guests might spend tomorrow, recipes for the dishes she was serving and descriptions of her favorite TV programs airing tonight.

Elizabeth barely tasted her food, and Sully barely looked at her.

Why, oh, why had she challenged him earlier? None of that was any of her business. Not his amnesia, not the mysterious fires, not the gold coins.

The fact that he kept kissing her had scrambled her brains but good.

After they brought their empty dinner dishes into the kitchen, Mrs. Butterfield invited them to join her in front of the television in the parlor. Elizabeth put on a smile and looked at Sully. "I've promised to help Chief Sullivan set up his laptop this evening. Would you like to do that now?"

"Why not," he said, his gaze meeting hers for the first time that night. It seemed...cool, and more distant than it had been before.

Damn. Had she blown it so badly?

She deliberately took his arm on the way to the stairs. "I'm sorry about earlier," she said. "It's really none of my affair, any of that."

He grunted noncommittally.

"I won't tell anyone about the gold."

"Doesn't matter. It's mine."

"Then you've started to remember?" she asked optimistically.

"Some things you never forget."

His words, spoken oddly like a censure, hung ominously between them as they climbed the stairs, giving her pause. What was that all about?

His jaw was clamped tight, his teeth gritted in pain by the time they reached his room. It was the third time he'd climbed the stairs that day and his leg was obviously bothering him. She helped him to the bed and took his cane as he sat.

"Can I get you anything? Do you have pain medication?"

"*Non.* Don't believe in opiates," he growled, rubbing the muscles. "I've seen what they can do to a man."

She smiled at his quaint term, but it quickly faded. Caleb hated drugs, too. Said they made him feel like he was wrapped in cotton batting. Unfortunately he had no choice. "Water, then?"

"I'm fine." It wasn't quite a growl this time, but he still didn't sound happy. Then he turned his attention fully on her, and said, "Elizabeth, you've been hiding something from me. I want to know what it is."

Her mouth dropped open at his harsh, pointed command. She'd been planning to tell him about Caleb, to ask him about being tested, as soon as the laptop was set up. But now she was almost afraid to broach the subject. His current mood did not appear exactly conducive to generous sacrifice on behalf of a stranger.

"Um…"

"The *truth,* Elizabeth. All of it."

Why did he look so suspicious?

"All right, fine," she said, sitting gingerly on the bed next to him. She put her hands in her lap and studied them. "The truth is, I came to South Carolina, to Magnolia Cove, specifically to find you."

He frowned. "Me? Why?"

"On behalf of my brother, Caleb. He has leukemia and needs a bone marrow transplant."

His suspicion turned to confusion. "I'm sorry, I don't know…I don't remember what that is." His uncertainty seemed genuine, mostly because the self-deprecating confession appeared to annoy him so much.

Swallowing a spurt of guilt, she briefly explained about the awful cancer and how it can sometimes be defeated with an infusion of healthy bone marrow, harvested from a compatible donor. The more she spoke, the more sympathetic his expression turned. Her hope soared.

"But why me?" he asked when she'd finished. He still seemed puzzled.

"Relatives are thirty percent more likely to be a match," she explained. "And you are very distantly related to my family. It's a long shot," she admitted. "But I'll do anything to help my brother. Even come all this way on a wild-goose chase."

He regarded her with a look she couldn't quite decipher.

"I know this is rotten timing," she hurried to say. "What with your accident and all. And I know your doctor will have the final say, so please don't answer me now. Just, if you would, talk to him…soon…and let me know what you decide. Either way, I'll be grateful if you would just consider it."

He continued to stare at her for a moment, then gave a curt nod. "Of course."

She couldn't help herself, she threw her arms around him and hugged him close. "Thank you. Oh, thank you! You have no idea how much this means to me."

He went suddenly stiff. "*Dieu*. Is that why you haven't wanted to kiss me? Because there is a family relationship between us? Are we cousins?"

She pulled back, shaking her head at his dismay. "Heavens, no! The relationship is generations distant. Besides, Caleb is not my biological brother. I was adopted."

"You were…adopted."

"There's no blood between us. I swear, not a drop."

The relief in Sully's expression was so obvious, her heart sang. Did his attraction to her run deeper than his reputation might suggest?

And yet, he made no move to return her hug. Or to kiss her.

Her cheeks warmed with a blush. "Sully, I was afraid to get close to you, physically," she said, looking down, "because I didn't want you to think I was trying to influence your decision by using, um…"

"Your body?"

She swallowed and nodded, her face scalding. "Exactly."

"That's it?" he murmured. "That's all you were hiding? No more secrets?"

"No secrets," she said. *Unlike you.* "Just a sick brother."

His lips whispered across her temple. His fingers grazed her waist. Caressed her gently, back and forth. She closed her eyes. Moments ticked by.

"What if," he said at last, his voice low, like the crunch of gravel, "what if I asked you for your body?"

Her breath sucked in. In shock.

She didn't move. Her hands still clutched his forearms, her thigh pressed snug up against his. His bare arms below his T-shirt sleeves were strong, corded; his jeans-clad thighs were hard with muscles. The masculine power of his body made her weaken with want.

But not like this. Not as part of a bargain.

And yet…if it was her only choice, for Caleb…

"That would depend," she whispered hoarsely, "on why you asked."

"If I promised to be tested, for this bone marrow thing, in exchange."

She swallowed again. Deeply, chokingly. "I would say yes."

His fingers found her chin and lifted, forcing her to meet his eyes. *"Donc,"* he said, looking fierce, "and if I asked as a man who simply wanted you? To make love to you and give you pleasure?"

For some inexplicable reason, she felt the sting of tears, pressing to come out. She forced them back. She wanted to say yes. She'd never wanted anything more in her life. But it felt…wrong. He'd mentioned pleasure, but she needed more than empty pleasure. When she let a man make love to her, she wanted it to mean something.

"I'd say no," she whispered.

For now, she wanted to add in haste, leaving open the possibility of the future, but she didn't. Not aloud. Because things were too complicated, and Andre Sullivan wasn't the kind of man to build a future around.

To her surprise, he gave her a crooked, sardonic smile. *"Quel dommage,* that I'm not a man to extort favors from desperate women, no matter how desirable."

She reached up and touched her fingers to his cheek. Understanding, to her relief, what he was saying. "Too bad I'm not a woman to give herself to every desirable man she meets, no matter how much she'd occasionally like to."

His eyebrow flicked. "It appears," he said, not without a hint of humor, "we've hit an impasse. I won't force you, and you won't surrender willingly."

She wouldn't put money on the latter, and was very glad he didn't push. She didn't know how long she could hold out against him. Already her blood felt like liquid lead in her veins, and she had a reckless urge to lean up and kiss him.

As though he could read her mind, his expression subtly changed. Then he leaned down and put his lips to hers. Barely touching, he halted, suspended, for an endless moment.

A low, needy sound floated through the silent room. With a start, she realized it had come from her own throat. Lord, did she want him that badly? She knew the answer without thinking.

Perhaps…perhaps she could allow herself just a kiss? Surely a kiss couldn't hurt, or be construed as undue influence. Was that what he was saying with his gentle invitation?

Sensing he would not move on his own, she threaded her fingers through his hair, drew him closer.

"Just a kiss," she whispered into his mouth. "Nothing further."

"Would you tease me?" he asked.

She could feel the barely leashed restraint in the muscles of his arms, of his thigh. She could see the blatant want growing large between his legs.

She was playing with fire. And this man was chief of the fire department.

"I'll stop if you want me to."

"Dieu, non. Jamais." Never.

So she opened her mouth, and slowly seduced him into the kiss with her tongue and her lips. Courting his response. Enflaming his need. It was the most quiveringly sensual thing she'd ever done.

She loved the taste of him, loved the feel of his firm flesh beneath her hands. Melted at the dusky, masculine smell of his skin and his hair and his desire for her.

She was in deep trouble, and she knew it.

She should stop this, stop their kiss. But she couldn't make herself. Not yet. Just a little more…

"Ma chère," he whispered. *"Ma douce."*

She shivered at his low-spoken love words, sensing a depth in them that defied a twenty-four-hour acquaintance. Thoughts of the old legend flitted through her mind, of the pirate and his lady. "Sully," she moaned softly. *Sullivan Fouquet?*

He gave an answering groan, and eased her back onto the mattress, canting over her, slipping his leg over hers. Not exactly trapping her, but…suggestively claiming her.

She tried to remember all the reasons why she shouldn't let him. But his lips, his mouth, were all too drugging. And then his hand lifted to join in the persuasion. He reached for the buttons of her blouse.

She covered his fingers with her own. "Just a kiss, remember?" she reminded him, her breath coming fast and shallow, her heart thumping hard.

"But you never said where," he pointed out.

"Lips. Mouth," she murmured, meeting his again.

"Breasts?" The stiff tip of his tongue met hers, teasing, enticing. In imitation of what he suggested.

Her nipples spiraled tightly and it was her turn to groan.

But her hapless sound of surrender was drowned in the sudden, sharp ring of the phone on the nightstand. They froze, their lips halting in midkiss. A siren wailed in the distance. And the foghorn-blast of a fire engine sounded.

The phone rang again.

Sully swore.

She frowned. "Would they call you?" she asked. "To a fire? On your first day out of the hospital?"

He swore again, rolled to his back and covered his eyes with the hand that had so recently targeted her buttons.

He still did not answer the persistent ringing. So she did. Prepared to inform them the chief was not fit enough to go back to work yet and they could just fight their fires without him for a while longer.

But when she started to say that, the man on the other end interrupted. "This is Jake Santee. Tell Chief Sullivan the fire's in an old historic building. Tell him it's the work of an arsonist. Tell him I think it's Wesley Peel."

Chapter 5

Merde.

This was the call Sully had been dreading, ever since learning of Andre Sullivan's occupation. He *hated* fire. *Really* hated it.

He could control the fear for small, contained blazes such as a lantern or fireplace. But when Elizabeth repeated what Jake Santee had told her, Sully knew he must face his worst fear sooner rather than later. A large, uncontrolled blaze.

He sat up, regretting the call even more for its untimely interruption. He gathered Elizabeth close. "If Jake thinks Peel has returned, I should go."

"Surely your doctor hasn't given you the go-ahead to suit up yet?"

"Don't worry. I have no intention of doing more than

observing." And that was for damned sure. He'd stay as far away from the fire as possible.

He lifted her chin and kissed her. Wanting nothing more than to tumble her to the mattress again and persuade her out of her clothes.

"Shall I drive you?" she asked.

He nodded. Maybe if he didn't let her out of his sight, they could pick up later where they'd left off.

"Tomorrow, I'll ask my doctor about the test for your brother," he said, rising from the bed. Then he caught her hand and added, "Regardless of what happens tonight."

She smiled, squeezing his fingers. "Thank you."

As it turned out, when they went out the front gate of the Pirate's Rest Inn they could already see smoke and flames shooting into the black sky from just a few blocks away. He talked her into walking with him instead of adding to the chaos of clogged curiosity-seeking traffic on the narrow village streets.

Hurrying down Fouquet Street, it didn't take Sully long to recognize which historic building was burning.

It was his old town house. The one he and Elizabeth had visited only hours before.

"Mon Dieu," he muttered, along with a choice swearword. A coincidence? Or had Peel been watching them the whole time?

"My God," Elizabeth said, her voice wavering. "Was he targeting Sullivan Fouquet's house, or was it a warning…for you?"

A question he'd dearly like to know the answer to.

He put an arm around her, glancing into the dark recesses of the alleyways and blank windows of closed businesses as they approached the jumble of police cars, fire trucks and ambulances that marked the perimeter of the fire scene. He concentrated on spotting Peel among the shifting shadows and the gaggle of onlookers. So he wouldn't fixate on the fire raging just a few hundred feet away.

But it was no use.

Like dancing devils, the flames leaped and licked at the row of ancient timber houses, consuming the structure with an ungodly roar and the acid stench of smoke and burning. Clouds of putrid steam rose as plumes of water from the hoses arced onto the blazing roof. Scorching heat rolled off the whole mess, blistering everything in its path.

Gooseflesh swept over Sully's skin and his stomach roiled. Boyhood memories of being caught in the bowels of a ship unable to get out, choking, screaming, roasting alive, assailed him. He turned his back to the flames and doubled over, gasping for a clean breath, battling the panic.

"Sully!" Elizabeth's worried call cut through the din of the fire and the men fighting it.

"Are you all right, Chief?" Jake Santee's voice joined hers.

"Fine," Sully said, straightening. Clenching his jaw. Turning back to face his terror. He'd survived it as a boy. And more recently the flames had brought him back to mortal life. Both miraculous. *He should not be afraid.*

"I'm fine," he repeated. "Just…"

Santee nodded, his eyes knowing. The eyes of a man who had been through it himself. "Take your time," he said. "And keep Miss Hamilton back here behind the line."

Sully nodded, sticking his hands in the back pockets of his jeans to keep them from shaking. Grateful to the other man for giving him a way to keep face and not look weak in front of his men. No matter that it was for the wrong reason.

"You think this is Peel's work?" Sully asked of him.

"Pretty sure of it," Jake said. "Fits his MO, and his obsession with that pirate treasure. I hear Sullivan Fouquet lived in this block in the late 1700s. But the place is empty now, so Peel couldn't have been looking for diaries or paintings like he did before. That's new."

"Not necessarily," Elizabeth said.

Jake turned to her in surprise. "How so?"

"Sully and I were here earlier. Inside the town house. There was a secret hidey-hole in one of the bedrooms. Maybe Peel knew about it and thought there was still something hidden there."

Jake frowned, looking from her to Sully. "You were inside?"

"I have a key," Sully explained, wishing Elizabeth hadn't brought it up. "A friend of mine owns the building. Since it's slated to be demolished—" he gave a shrug "—he wanted me to go through and make sure everything had been removed."

"A friend. Who?" Jake asked, his brow beetling.

"James Tyler. He's abroad on his honeymoon."

Jake's eyes narrowed consideringly. "Tyler? The antiques dealer? The man whose wife you rescued?"

"He's the one."

Tyree had told him a bit about Jake Santee, because he was a good friend of Andre Sullivan's. Jake had been racked with guilt over Sully's massive injuries—as well as Clara and Tyree's—blaming himself because Jake had known ahead of time Peel might be setting that fire. But he'd always been just a little suspicious of Tyree's—James Tyler's—real interest in the arson cases.

"Hmm."

"Don't even think it, Jake," Sully said. "Tyler had nothing to do with the fire tonight. Or any of the others."

Jake held up his hands. "I know, I know. Tyler getting shot was evidence enough. Not to mention him being a thousand miles away by now. But I still feel like something hinky's going on with him. There's a connection I'm not seeing."

He had no idea.

"I guess this means the case is reopened?" Sully asked.

"Absolutely."

Suddenly there was a commotion and shouts as a half-dozen men came scrambling out of the burning building. "Everyone get back! It's coming down!"

"Get out of here!" Jake yelled, then took off at a run to help. "We'll talk tomorrow."

A few seconds later a rumbling began, and before their eyes, what was left of the town houses fell in on itself, erupting in a whoosh of sparks and flame.

Sully didn't know how it happened, but when it was over he found himself sprawled on the ground, clutching Elizabeth under him in a death-grip, his arms wrapped protectively around her.

"You hurt?" he cautiously asked when he dared lift his head.

"I'm good," she answered. "You?"

"Bien." He closed his eyes, took a deep, steadying breath.

"It's okay, you know."

He opened his eyes again and looked down at her. "What is?"

"To be afraid. A fire almost killed you, Sully. If it were me, I'd be terrified. No way would you get me within a mile of another one."

An ironic smile teased his lips. "Yeah, but I'm the fire chief, *chère*. Kinda goes with the territory."

"So quit."

"My men look to me for leadership. I can't let them down."

Her fingers tunneled gently in his hair. She smiled up at him. "You're a good man, Andre Sullivan."

Just then, a group of loud, brassy men in grimy fire-fighters gear tromped by. One of them spotted them lying on the ground and halted with a chortle. "Dang, Chief!" he called out good-naturedly. "Leave it to you to find the prettiest gal in the crowd to rescue. That's not the same one as this morning, is it?"

The rest of the men laughed and waved, then they all clomped along, heading for one of the huge red engines. But when Sully glanced back down at Elizabeth, she wasn't laughing.

"Guess we are a bit conspicuous in this position," she said tightly, and shoved a hand against his shoulder so he rolled unceremoniously off her. She scrambled to her feet and brushed off her skirt and blouse. "Need a hand up?"

"I'll manage." Inwardly he cursed his men's rude comments as he groped for his walking stick and pushed awkwardly to his feet. Knowing Andre Sullivan's reputation, they'd probably done it on purpose—helping their confirmed bachelor captain establish solid boundaries with his newest conquest. *You might have him now, baby, but tomorrow he'll be gone.* His lack of staying power with Lisa Grosvenor must have confirmed that opinion.

Sully's stomach wrenched. Obviously Elizabeth had heard the message loud and clear. She was standing watching the remnants of the fire burn out with her arms crossed rigidly under her breasts, her face red as the flames.

Le Bon Dieu, mait la main. God help him.

"Chère," he said softly, reaching out to touch a blond tendril that had blown across her cheek. "Don't listen to them. That Andre Sullivan, the one they knew, he's gone…changed. I'm just not that man anymore."

She nodded, but her smile was strained. "It doesn't really matter," she said. "I have no designs on your…freedom. I'll only be here a few days, until your doctor decides whether you can donate bone marrow or not."

The reminder of why she was in Magnolia Cove swept through him like a cooling wind. It couldn't be denied, she wanted something from him. A noble something, as far as he could tell, but still something she treasured beyond price. Something for which she was even willing to sacrifice her virtue—to sleep with him when she otherwise wouldn't.

If his guess about the pencil drawing was correct, Elizabeth Hayden had wanted something from him, too. Something she treasured more than her virtue—wealth. Had she sacrificed herself to him to get it? Had her love simply been a sham? Had she playacted her affections for him for all that time, in order to put her hands on the greater prize?

The new Elizabeth had readily revealed her reasons for seeking him out and maintained she held no other secrets than a sick brother. Indeed what could they possibly be? She had been forthcoming, even in terms of her willingness to bargain with her favors.

Maybe it was the hated smell of smoke in his nostrils, or the heat of the flame on his skin that was causing this bout of paranoia. But suddenly, he was unsure of her, too.

He'd been so certain Elizabeth Hayden had somehow come back to life, to be with him, as Elizabeth Hamilton. But if he was right, was the present Elizabeth also out to betray him? If so, how?

He needed to find out. Before he did anything foolish. Or got in deeper. He needed a plan.

A plan that would reveal her true purpose.

A determined smile sketched itself across his face. Because he knew just the way.

When they arrived back at the Pirate's Rest Inn, Sully pulled open the front door for Elizabeth, and asked, "Will you still help me with the laptop? I know it's getting late, but I really should send a message to my friend. About his building burning down. Unfortunately I have no idea how."

Being in the same room with Andre Sullivan was the

last thing Elizabeth wanted at the moment, but when put that way she could hardly refuse.

"Sure," she said, and went inside.

She had to pull herself together. Her emotions were all over the map. She'd never met a man before who brought out such contradictory feelings in her—one minute convinced he was nothing but a bounder interested only in her body, the next, not really sure if she cared. Being held in his arms made her forget everything except how good it felt to be there. Made her want things she'd never wanted before.

Being with Caleb for every waking hour she didn't spend working on the farm and her job, she hadn't given herself a chance to dream about falling in love or having a family of her own. Being with Sully changed all that.

Damn, she needed some distance from the man.

Except, for Caleb's sake she had to stick close to him, to help convince him to do the bone marrow transplant, if he proved to be a match. If she avoided him, he might think she didn't care about his answer.

Which she did. More than anything.

Enough to allow him to be interested only in her body, if that's what he wanted?

Oh, Lord.

What had possessed her to tell him she'd say yes?

That wasn't her, wasn't what she was like. It wasn't what Caleb would want her to do, either.

And yet, there was a different, hidden side to Sully that she was slowly getting to know. A vulnerable side that seemed stuck in another, simpler time; an honorable side willing to face his inner demons rather than disappoint the men who looked up to him. A romantic side that gazed at her with such longing it made her weak in the knees.

And nothing appealed to her more than the idea of making love to that more sensitive, admirable side of him.

Andre Sullivan was certainly a man of vast contradictions.

But he wasn't interested in making love, an inner voice warned her. All he wanted was sex. *To give her pleasure.*

Or...*had* the accident really changed him?

They had reached the second-floor landing in front of her door. He stopped and gazed up the stairs as though he'd rather face a firing squad than take that last flight up to his room.

"You're about to fall over. Why don't we set up your laptop in my room for now?" she suggested. "By the time you've sent your e-mail you'll have caught your breath and can make it up to the third floor without killing yourself."

He sent her a look. "Have I mentioned how much I hate this?" he muttered.

"Once or twice." With a commiserating grin, she held out her palm. "Give me your key. I'll get the computer."

Which she did. By the time she'd gotten back to her room, he was stretched out on the bed with his eyes closed.

She quietly set down the laptop. "Sully?" she whispered, not wanting to wake him if he was asleep. He must be exhausted.

No answer.

She approached, taking in the sight of him. He was

such an incredibly handsome man. Tall and well-built, broad-shouldered and brawny, his body nearly filled up all the available space on her bed. His face bore the creases and angles of his outdoor life and his optimistic personality, the sculpted curve of his lips his innate sensuality.

To give her pleasure... Hell, he was a man custom-made to give a woman pleasure. She shivered at the thought of being that woman.

Would it be so wrong to give in to this one, small indiscretion? It had been so long....

She stepped back and turned, squelching the impulse to join him in her bed. She could switch rooms with him for the night. That would remove the all-too-real temptation.

But first she plugged in the laptop and got the e-mail up and running. The bright blue and yellow screen popped up and before she could react, the speaker chirped brightly, "You've got mail!"

She winced as Sully stirred.

"Elizabeth?" His voice was deep and rough with sleep.

"I'm here."

"Sorry, I must have dozed off." He made to sit up.

"No, stay where you are. I'll sleep in your bed tonight."

His eyes sought hers, brow raised. "The hell, you say. I'll be damned if I finally get you into my bed and am not there to enjoy it."

She smiled. "You have a reassuringly one-tracked mind, Chief Sullivan."

The other brow hiked. "Reassuringly?"

"For a few minutes there I thought you might really

have changed. It's so much easier to resist a slimy skirt-chaser."

"You wound me," he said, his lips turning down in a moue. He flopped back on the pillow.

"You know I'm joking."

"Aye. But not really. That's what you think of me, and to be sure, every bit of evidence points to the truth of it. The problem is, the evidence is all from before the accident."

"True." Could a near-death experience really change a man's inner core? But...if for whatever reason he was faking his amnesia...was this just an act?

"Give me a chance, Elizabeth," he urged. "The *new* me."

Suddenly she realized what was bothering her more than anything else.

"Why?" she asked. "Why do you want me to give you a chance? Why not just take what I once offered with just that one string attached, that you plan to do anyway?"

And if he said a single word about Sullivan Fouquet and his tragic fiancée, Elizabeth, she would walk right out the door. Not because it would prove he was crazy, but because she wanted to be wanted for *herself,* not that she reminded him of some far-fetched figment of his imagination.

Though, crazy...yeah, crazy would be bad, too.

"Why do I want you?" His gaze raked over her. "Join me in this bed and I'll show you why."

She tipped her head, disappointed. "Your argument is a circular one. I'm not denying our chemistry, Sully. I'm pretty sure sex with you would be incredible. But you're trying to convince me you're not interested in meaningless sex. Joining you in bed doesn't seem the answer."

"Who said anything about meaningless?" The corner of his mouth crooked up. "At least lie down here next to me while we discuss it."

The man was truly incorrigible. "Sully…"

"I kept my promise last night, didn't I?"

She had to admit he had. As far as it went. If the phone hadn't rung, though…

He scooted to one side and patted the mattress next to him. *"Vien."*

And there was another thing that bothered her. The Cajun accent and French words. He'd even stopped correcting himself when he used them.

"Lizzie?"

She'd probably live to regret it.

She knew darn well she wasn't strong enough to resist him if he genuinely tried to seduce her.

But she also knew she'd kick herself for the rest of her life if she didn't make up her mind and resolve this insane situation one way or another.

She was an adult. If she wanted to sleep with the man, she would sleep with him. If she didn't, well, then she wouldn't. But she would do neither out of fear—fear of talking things out. Fear of learning what he really wanted of her.

"All right," she said, and slipped out of her shoes. He hadn't made it easy. He'd moved to the near side of the bed, forcing her to climb over him to get to the empty side.

She supposed it was that playing with fire thing

again, but for some unfathomable reason, it pushed a button with her. She took up his challenge.

Deliberately she slid her body over his, letting her breasts and thighs brush against his chest and hips, and the ends of her long hair trail over his mouth.

All at once his hands grasped her around the ribs, stopping her movement, holding her fast above him. Unafraid, she looked down into his smoldering eyes.

Her hands were to either side of his head, her knees bent outside his thighs, but he'd taken complete control of her with his powerful grip. Slowly he lowered her so the tips of her breasts once again brushed over his chest. He moved her, a fraction of an inch, then back again. Her nipples zinged with electric sensation, sending curls of aching want straight to her center. Then he did it again.

Neither of them spoke, but his gauntlet was so deliberate and obvious there was no need. The only question was, what was she going to do about it?

Was this what they meant by eyes wide open?

"Why?" she repeated, her throat tight with desire for him. Unwilling to give in without an answer.

"Because you want me. And I want you."

"That's—" she swallowed, lied "—not good enough."

He let her slip down a little in his grip, so her breasts pillowed into his chest. So their mouths were nearly touching. So his lengthening, hardening arousal pressed provocatively between her legs.

"Non?"

"No," she affirmed.

"Because you want more."

"Yes. No. I—I don't know."

"Because you want more," he repeated softly, "but you don't trust me. Or—"

He spun them over and she landed under him, his tall, hard frame pushing her deep into the feather bed. She gasped, grappling with the strong hands that captured her wrists and held.

"Or perhaps," he continued, "you hesitate because you feel guilty."

She stilled her struggles at his words, staring up at him. "It's true, I would feel guilty asking you to go through another painful medical procedure," she said, "if it turns out you're a match for Caleb." She swallowed again, heavily. "But that wouldn't keep me from sleeping with you. If anything…" She halted the thought before it could escape.

His brows arched elegantly. "Out of pity? Really, Elizabeth, you insult me now."

"Not pity," she murmured contritely. "Comfort. Ease. Gratitude." She exhaled. "Heartfelt gratitude."

He studied her from above, his eyes black, inscrutable. "Nothing more?"

The blood in her veins seemed to thicken, the strength in her limbs to desert her. Her heart thudded fast in her chest as his relentless gaze refused to release her.

"Yes," she whispered. "Desire."

"Desire for what, *chère?*"

"To feel you inside me."

Chapter 6

It was all the invitation Sully needed.

He was satisfied she was hiding nothing from him, but even if he weren't, it had been too long and he wanted her too badly to stop now.

He covered her mouth with his and kissed her. Kissed her hard and deep, until he felt the melting of her limbs beneath him and heard her moans of surrender.

"Why do I want you?" he murmured, lifting so he could see the need in her half-lidded eyes and the flare of her nostrils, the blush of desire on her cheeks. "Because you're mine, Elizabeth. I recognized it the moment I saw you. It's no use fighting fate. You belong with me."

He let her wrists go and reached for her blouse. Her hand covered his as he went for the buttons.

"You thought I was someone else when you first saw me, Sully. But I'm not her, and I don't want—"

"A mistake," he interrupted, swiftly undoing the top buttons. "She betrayed me, *chère*. In the past. Pretended to be something she wasn't, to feel something she didn't. But you would never do that, *non?*"

"Of course not!"

He lost patience, and with a quick yank, ripped her blouse open. Buttons flew everywhere. She gasped as he put his lips to the slope of her breast and feasted on her lush flesh. Shoving aside the lacy garment that covered it, he took her pebbled nipple in his mouth and suckled deeply.

Her body bowed under him and he groaned with the powerful, grinding want that coursed through him from his toes to the roots of his hair. It had been so damned long....

His senses filled with her, with the sweet womanly scent of her, the silken feel of her soft curves, the taste of her on his tongue. The needy moans...

He tugged uselessly at the scrap of lace. "Take it off," he ordered, pulling her upright to peel off her blouse. In a twinkling he had her skirt off and the rest as well, so she was finally naked in his arms.

"*Si belle,*" he murmured, the words clogging his throat at the sight of her pale beauty. "You take my breath away."

She twined her arms around his neck and smiled shyly as her lips met his. "Your turn," she whispered.

"*Mais,* yeah," he answered, his voice low and husky. "I fully intend to take your breath away...and more than once."

* * *

Elizabeth had never been made love to as Sully made love to her. With his tongue he swept away every doubt, every hesitation, every thought of ease or gratitude. With his lips he breathed life into her body, which had up until this moment lain dormant, waiting for this man to awaken it. With his touch, he convinced her that all he said was true.

She belonged with him.

With slow, sure moves, he kissed and licked and touched her everywhere. For blissful hours he learned her body inch by inch, lingering in all the places that made her shiver and quake in pleasure.

He took her breath away. More than once.

And then he came inside her, thrusting into her, filling her to bursting with his thick, hard length. And took her breath away again.

Afterward, as she lay under him, dizzy with the last tremors of passion and panting with extravagant completion, she knew she would never be the same again.

How was it possible to fall so far so fast?

He scraped the damp hair from her brow and gazed down at her so tenderly, her heart simply melted in her chest.

"C'est bon?"

She smiled, not caring if her feelings were as transparent as glass. "More than good. Incredible."

She loved the weight of him on top of her, loved the feel of his thighs resting between hers, loved the hot stickiness of their skin pressed together, loved the fact that he was still half aroused as he reposed within her, sated.

It was as carnal a position as she'd ever been in. With a man she barely knew. She should feel mortified, embarrassed, or at the very least slightly guilty. But she felt none of that.

What she felt was happy. And content. And thoroughly loved.

Which was the biggest piece of self-delusion she'd entertained in her life. But right now she didn't care. She only wanted to savor the exotic and unfamiliar feelings.

"Shall I stay or go?" he asked softly, spooning up close against her back after disposing of the protection he'd fumbled with earlier as though it had been his first time. *So endearing.*

"Don't you dare leave," she murmured, closing her eyes, wrapping her arms over his, already drifting off.

He kissed her hair. "Sleep, then. I'll be right here when you wake."

With a sigh, she nestled closer to him. And slept, long and soundly. Better than she'd slept since Caleb was diagnosed with leukemia. Better than she had since her mother and father died in the car crash. Better than she had, well, ever in her life.

And when she awoke, he was…
Gone.

"Impossible."

Sully stared in bald disbelief at the computer screen in Jake Santee's office at the Magnolia Cove Fire Department. "There must be something wrong with the blasted thing!"

Sully had forgotten all about his physical therapy appointment this morning. He hadn't had the heart to wake Elizabeth, who was still sleeping peacefully well after the sun rose, so he'd left a note and sneaked out to see if any of the guys from the Magnolia Cove station could drive him to Old Fort Mystic Medical Center. Jake had volunteered, since he was headed in that direction anyway. He maintained an office at both fire stations.

"You're the one who wanted to know," Jake told him patiently, peering at the computer screen, but only succeeded in making Sully's blood pound harder in his veins. "Trust me, credit bureaus and the Department of Motor Vehicles don't lie."

At the medical center, Sully had asked his doctor about Elizabeth's request. The doctor had seen no problem with the preliminary compatibility test itself, which was a simple blood test, but had several reservations about the harvesting procedure, should Sully prove a match. His body had gone through a lot already. It may be too soon to ask more of it. Then the doctor had asked about his family relationship with Caleb, but Sully hadn't been able to answer.

When Jake picked him up again, they'd driven back and hung around Jake's office for a while, talking about the fire last night. Noticing the computer on the arson investigator's desk, Sully remembered that Tyree was always saying how you could find out anything in the world with a computer. So he'd asked Jake to do some quick research into Caleb and Elizabeth's family tree. They were now looking at the results.

He clenched his jaw, anger coursing through his entire being. "Are you *sure?*"

Sully was still suspicious of the whole computer thing. He'd seen plenty of them in the hospital, of course, so he was familiar with the general concept. But it seemed incredible to him that all that information could be instantly retrieved from a tiny box not even as big as a sea chest.

"Positive," Jake assured him. "So what's the problem? You already knew you were distantly related to the Connecticut Sullivans, right?"

Oh, yeah. He knew.

To the depths of his soul he knew.

To the gates of hell and back he knew.

And he'd been plucked from the dead to wreak his revenge on them and sever that connection, finishing it forever. To fulfill the curse he himself had put on the line so long ago.

But Elizabeth... *Elizabeth* was a Sullivan?

It couldn't be! She'd sworn she had no more secrets. That her name was Hamilton. And yet here was the worst secret she could possibly have kept from him!

His lover had been brought up in the lair of the old devil himself—with Sully's mortal enemy as her brother.

Mon Dieu! The irony!

He had bedded the enemy's sister! And she had asked him to save the very person he'd sworn to see consigned to the lowest depths of hell—the last living male heir to Lord Henry Sullivan.

Lord Henry—the man who had cold-bloodedly murdered Sully's family.

Chapter 7

"Chief? Chief?"

Sully dragged himself from the swift tempest of his rage and forced a neutral expression to his face. "Aye? Sorry, I was lost at sea for a moment."

Jake hiked a brow. "Didn't know you sailed."

"I'm a ship's cap—" Sully suddenly remembered who he was now. "I mean, I'd like to learn—" And that Jake was probably jesting. *Merde.* "What was it you wanted?"

The other man grinned. "Lunchtime, Captain. Feel like grabbing a bite?"

Sully's anger howled from its confinement. "Not today, Jake. I've got a few things I need to take care of."

He declined Jake's offer of a ride, swiped up the printout of Elizabeth's family tree and his walking stick, then stalked out of the station.

He needed to be alone. To tame his savage thoughts before confronting Elizabeth.

Casting about for somewhere to go where he wouldn't be disturbed, his gaze went instinctively in the direction of his favorite pub, the Moon and Palmetto. Bad idea. He and Tyree had danced their fatal duel on the Moon and Palmetto's already ancient floorboards two hundred years earlier. Aye, and three months ago it had burned down, taking Andre Sullivan with it and spitting Sully out of its dying flames like a phoenix rising to life again.

Just as well it was gone. Bad mojo there.

Clenching his jaw, he set off with no direction in mind. And in less than five minutes found himself storming up the front walk to the Pirate's Rest Inn.

So much for letting off steam.

"There you are, Chief Sullivan!" Mrs. Butterfield sang out from a rocking chair on the front porch when she spotted him. "Miss Hamilton and I missed you at breakfast! How did your doctor's appointment go?"

"Just fine, ma'am, thank you for asking," he said politely through a stiff smile. "And where is Miss Hamilton?"

"Sully!" The screen door opened and she stepped through it looking pretty as a spring morning, her duplicitous eyes sparkling with cheer, her lying mouth curved up in a smile of welcome as she reached for him. As soon as she saw his face, she faltered, her hand suspended in midair. "What's wrong? Did the doctor—"

"*You.* Come with me." He seized her hand, slung open the door and towed her roughly inside. "Excuse us, Miz Butterfield," he called over his shoulder.

"Sully, what—"

He turned to Elizabeth, and growled, "*Arrête.* Not a word."

He had no memory of how he got up the stairs so quickly, barely noticed the pain lancing through his leg. When they reached her room he shoved her inside, slammed the door and pushed her back up against it. He smacked his hands onto the solid wood on either side of her head and her blue eyes went wide. With shock, not fear, he noted perversely, at the one moment of her life when she should fear him most ardently.

"*Why?*" he demanded, his voice sharp as a blade. "Why did you not tell me?"

Her gaze flickered. Her hands crept toward his chest. "Tell you what? Sully, why are you—"

"Don't!" Before she could touch him, he seized her wrists and pinioned them above her head. "Do not pretend you don't know—"

"But I don't! Please…"

He clenched his jaw, restraining his wrath by a thread. "You should have told me you are a Sullivan, Elizabeth."

"But I—" Confusion swept across her face. "I—I'm not, really. I'm a Hamilton. Yes, the Sullivans adopted me, but— Why on earth would it matter?"

"It *matters,*" he roared.

She jumped. Fear finally began to pool in her eyes. Her hands trembled in his grip.

"Okay. I'm sorry," she said shakily. "I wasn't trying to hide anything, honest."

He searched her face, her soul. He was so damned angry. All he could think of since seeing her name on that computer screen, linked with that of his hated nemesis, was that he'd been right. She *had* betrayed him. She'd known all along, had used him and hurt him deliberately.

"Sully?"

It was the pleading in her open, guileless gaze that finally got through to him.

Non. God's Teeth. Of course she didn't know.

His fury notched down. Just a little.

How could she know? She had no idea who he was. Who he *really* was—or what had happened to his family. No one knew…no one but Tyree. It was part of the Sullivan Fouquet mystique.

He didn't let her loose, but bent his head and glared down at the floor, composing himself. He had to say…something. He must offer some manner of explanation for his bizarre behavior. And then he had to crush her hopes.

Because despite her innocence, there was not a chance in Hades that he would help her brother, a Sullivan.

"Sully? Talk to me, sweetheart."

The endearment nearly gutted him. He recalled all they had shared last night. All the dreams he had spun for a future that could make up for everything he'd been denied in the past…

Abruptly he dropped her wrists. Turned his back and paced away.

"I can't do it," he said.

She was silent for a long moment, then sighed. He

didn't dare turn, couldn't bear to see the hurt in *her* eyes, the betrayal in *her* face.

"I know," she murmured. "Though I hadn't expected it quite so soon...." Her voice wavered. "Guess it's better this way." He heard the doorknob turn. "But...I'm hoping you won't let it affect your answer about the test."

He jerked around, realizing she had misinterpreted. "*Non,* you don't understand. I'm *talking* about the test. Not—" He took a step toward her, then halted. If he touched her, he'd be lost. "I will not help your brother. I cannot."

Her crestfallen face paled with a far greater distress. "The doctor said no?"

Sully squared his stance. Better to face the truth. "*I'm* saying no."

Her brow pleated in incomprehension. "But...why?"

His brain spun with the portent of the moment.

Because this was the fulfillment of a whole lifetime lived for one single purpose—revenge. This was the fruition of the curse Sully himself had placed on the man who had brutally ripped the life from his beloved parents and destroyed his family and his childhood.

Caleb was the last of his line. The very last. Only when he was cold in the ground would Sully's own parents' deaths be avenged.

"Because he's a Sullivan," Sully gritted out, knowing there was no way she would ever understand. And there was no way he could ever explain.

"But you're a Sullivan, too," she argued, voice wavering.

"Not by choice," he shot back. Then reined in his fury. "I'm sorry, Elizabeth. It is not within my power to offer aid or even hope to my enemy."

"Enemy? What are you talking about?"

He closed his eyes—how to begin?—then opened them again. "Let's just say your family and my family have a terrible history. Things were done in the past. Unforgivable things."

Elizabeth's jaw slackened. "But… How far in the past? Sully, my family didn't even know about your branch until last week!" Her eyes widened. "Oh, God, please tell me this is not a Civil War thing. I know you Southerners are—"

He held up a hand. He wasn't sure what she was referring to, but one thing was certain. "This is not about a war. It's personal. Very personal."

She stared at him. "What, then? Whatever it is, we can fix it together. We're…friends, at least…aren't we? That's a start." Tears suddenly filled her eyes. "Sully, please. I'm begging you."

He had to gird himself against reaching for her. What a damnable position! Ruthlessly, he cut off the impulse to weaken.

"Non. The matter is closed." He strode to the door and swung it open. Took one last look at the woman he would give anything—*almost anything*—to hold in his arms again. "I'm sorry," he said again.

And the pain of that truth would have broken his heart if only the pain of an earlier truth hadn't already done such a thorough job.

* * *

Stunned, Elizabeth watched the door shut on Sully's imposing figure.

What the hell had just happened?

Of all the possible scenarios she expected to be playing out with him this morning, this was bottom of the list. No, this wouldn't even have *made* the list.

Enemy? Family history? What was he talking about?

Groping for the bed, she lay down and tried to control her trembling body. *She couldn't do this.*

The emotional roller coaster she'd been on for the past few weeks was too much to bear.

Caleb's sure and steady decline had been awful to witness, but when his doctor had finally warned that unless he got a bone marrow transplant soon it could be too late, that's when the reality of the situation had finally hit Elizabeth hard. Her brother was going to die. Friends, family, the donor register had all been exhausted. There was no one left to turn to.

And then a miracle had happened. She'd found a reference in some old family papers about the Carolina Sullivans. Barely scraping together the cost of a ticket south, she'd managed to find Andre Sullivan. Then came the crushing news that Andre had been close to death himself, and only now was out of the hospital.

But then a second miracle had happened: he'd seemed amenable to helping Caleb. Not only that, Elizabeth had fallen for the man. Hook, line and sinker. She'd given her body to him. And her heart. A few hours ago, for the first time in years, she'd been glowing with happiness. Positive everything—*everything*—would turn out well.

But suddenly now…now this. The worst shock yet. He'd changed his mind. About *both* her and the transplant. For the most idiotic of reasons—no reason at all, that she could see.

She could—just—absorb the blow his personal rejection struck to the inner reaches of her heart. But the fact that he was actually willing to let Caleb die over some ancient, long-forgotten feud was too much to bear.

Terrible family history? Was he kidding? What could possibly be so horrible to turn a good man away from doing what he knew was right?

Or had she sadly misjudged him and his sense of honor?

Her breath hitched in a soft sob.

What would she do?

Oh, God, what would she do?

Half an hour later, Elizabeth sat up and dried her eyes. Having a good cry had helped. Enormously. She hadn't cried for ages and ages. Not since her adoptive father's funeral three years ago. Once in a while it did a body good to just let go and give in to the despair.

But enough was enough. Crying was not going to solve the problem at hand.

She'd gotten this far, damn it, and she had no intention of giving up now. Not until the last stone had been overturned and the last possibility to help her brother utilized.

Which meant Sully.

He was going to have that test come hell or high water!

She went into the bathroom and splashed her face with cold water. Reaching for a towel, she looked at the mirror, into the eyes of a woman she barely recognized, so different from the one who'd been there this morning—a woman brimming with adoration and optimism. Now both crushed.

Tears threatened anew, but she forced them back. The time for tears had passed. It was time for action.

Determinedly she fetched her cell phone and dialed her home number.

"Hello?"

Elizabeth's heart wrenched at Caleb's softly spoken greeting. He was home from the hospital? That could only mean one of two things. Either he was getting better, or…

She swallowed down the last thought. "Hi, honey. It's me. How are you doing, sweetie?"

"Bethy! I'm doing good. The doctor let me come home! How's your vacation?"

She and her mom, Gilda, hadn't told him the true reason for her trip. No sense getting his hopes up…

"It's been great, buddy. You wouldn't believe how different it is down here. All palm trees and ocean breezes."

"Sounds relaxing. You are relaxing like you're s'posed to be, aren't you?"

"Doing my best, Squirt."

"Meet any nice guys yet?"

For a second she couldn't breathe. It was an ongoing joke between them. For the past year or so he'd been playing matchmaker from his hospital bed, insisting she didn't go out on enough dates because she was always watching over him. She'd always insisted none of the guys she knew met her high standards.

"Well?" he prodded.

He'd gotten even more determined lately, since the doctor let slip that the drugs and chemo might affect his ability to have kids of his own later on. But Elizabeth was even more worried he was trying to find someone to fill her life when he wasn't there any longer....

"Tons," she choked out. "And these Southern guys sure are cute."

Caleb snickered. "But can they cook?"

"Very funny." Elizabeth laughed through the pain in her heart. She was notoriously untalented in the kitchen. Even Caleb boiled water better than she did.

They talked for a long time before she finally asked, "Is Mom around?"

A few moments later, Gilda came on the line with an effusive greeting. It felt so good to hear her mom's voice, her own cracked a little.

There was a pause, and Gilda said, "Caleb, dear, let me speak to your sister now." After he hung up, she said softly, "What's wrong, darling?"

Elizabeth had meant to be strong, really she had. Her mom did not need to hear all the sordid details of her foolhardiness concerning Sully, nor the gut-wrenching impasse they had come to about him having the bone marrow test. But she'd never been able to hide anything from the perceptive woman who'd loved her through thick and thin.

So it all came pouring out. All of it. She knew Gilda would never judge her, but offer support and a fresh perspective on things. After she was finished, Gilda pushed out a long, thoughtful breath.

"Wow. So, you're saying this Andre Sullivan believes

there was bad blood between the different branches of our families?"

"He's adamant, Mom. You should have seen his face when he talked about it. Pure hatred. It was scary."

"Did he threaten you?" she asked worriedly.

"No, nothing like that. He was furious, but only because he thought I'd hidden the truth from him."

"But he believes you now?"

"I'm sure he does."

"And yet, because of this mythical feud, he doesn't want to continue your relationship."

"That doesn't matter, Mom. What's important is that I talk him into taking the test. Otherwise, Caleb…" Her words trailed off as the impossible loomed, too ominous to bear.

After a short silence, her mom said, "I think they both matter. Darling, you hang in there. I'm going to look into this and find out what he's referring to. There must be some book or journal in Dad's library that will shed some light."

Don Sullivan had been inordinately proud of his vast collection of books, documents, paintings and photos that chronicled the lengthy and illustrious history of the Sullivan family. Their aristocratic forefathers had not come over on the *Mayflower,* but pretty soon thereafter. They'd acquired the estate through royal bequest by King Charles II in 1663, and there had been Sullivans living and working the lands ever since. Nowadays the remaining acres were just a tiny speck on the map compared to what their domain had once been, but her adoptive father had always said it was the Sullivan name and their honorable heritage that were important, not how much land they owned.

Of course, Elizabeth's birth family, the Hamiltons, were distantly connected to one of the Founding Fathers and assorted other dignitaries, so she understood his pride of lineage. It was a shame that it would all end with Caleb, if the doctors were right about him not being able to have children.

All at once an appalling thought occurred to her. "Mom, if Caleb..." She took a deep breath. "I know the entailment laws concerning old heritage properties are complicated. Is there any way Andre Sullivan might be in line to inherit the Connecticut estate?"

She could almost hear the gears turning in her mom's head. "Do you think that's what he's—"

"No!" Elizabeth cut off the repugnant thought. "I don't. But..." If she had misjudged Sully... "Maybe it wouldn't hurt to find out."

"I agree. But from what you've said, it doesn't sound to me like your Sully is the kind of man who could be that ruthless or dishonest."

Then again, her mom hadn't seen the look on his face. On the other hand, she was quite certain that look had had nothing to do with money or wealth.

"I hope you're right. But, Mom," she reminded her gently "he's not my Sully."

Gilda sniffed. "Darling, I know you. You'd never have let things go as far as they have if the man didn't return your feelings. Trust me, this is just a temporary glitch. It'll all work out."

Her mom, the romantic. Could you tell she grew up in the sixties?

"But the first thing we need to do," Gilda continued,

"is learn what we can about this supposed feud. Clearing that up should solve everything quite nicely."

Elizabeth smiled. She was so glad she'd spilled her guts. She felt a thousand times better now that Gilda was helping. "Wish there were something I could do from here."

"There is one thing that's puzzling me…"

"What's that?"

"If Sully has amnesia, like you say, then…where is this coming from? He doesn't remember what leukemia is, or how to drive a car, but he remembers a family rift so old that our side has forgotten all about it?"

Elizabeth blinked. And sat up ramrod straight as a sudden, unbelievable thought occurred to her.

Ah, hell.

When she'd told Gilda about Sully, she'd omitted one small detail. She hadn't thought it was relevant. But…what if it was? What if…

She cleared her throat. "Mom, while you're doing your research, can you check out something for me?"

"Of course, darling. What?"

"I'd like to know if there is any mention of a certain name in connection to our family. Any connection at all to this person, no matter how remote or improbable."

"Sure. Who is it?"

"An eighteenth-century pirate. Sullivan Fouquet."

Pacing back and forth across the length of his room, Sully fought to contain the turmoil still rampant within his battered heart.

It had been three hours since he'd deserted Elizabeth.

Three hours since he'd looked right through her wretch-ed disappointment, ignored her pleading, thrown her affections in her shocked face and walked out.

He felt like a bastard.

Now that he'd calmed down, he realized none of this was her fault. She wasn't even a Sullivan. If it weren't for her blasted adopted brother... But she obviously loved the blighter.

So, there was nothing he could do. Besides, even if he were inclined to—which he most definitely was not—nothing could change the curse he had placed upon the Sullivans. Tyree's plight had proven Sully's voudou was powerful and irreversible once set in motion. Lord Henry's family was well and truly doomed to extinction.

"And good riddance to them," he growled, slashing a hand through his hair.

In nightmares he still heard his mother's screams for mercy, plain as the day they'd dragged his father to the stately old oak in front of the Sullivan manor house, where Lord Henry had slung a rope over a thick branch, tied in a noose.

"Leave him be!" she'd screamed at the devil, whose ears remained deaf to her pleading. "I'll come to you whenever you bid! I'll do as you wish, only don't harm my husband!"

It had taken two strong men to restrain her, and three to subdue Sully, who'd fought like a feral, thirteen-year-old wildcat to get to her and to save his father. Tears and dirt had streaked his face, his clothes were shredded from the struggle. But the worst was hearing his mother beg. And learning the bitter truth of her disgrace—and his.

"Please!" she'd screamed as Lord Henry lifted up his great, black boot one last time. "For God's sake! *For the sake of your son!*"

And in that one terrible, awful moment, Sully's world had been kicked out from under him just as surely as the stool shot from beneath his father's feet.

Chapter 8

It had been a hell of a revelation for a young boy, hearing he'd been the product of rape. But as Sully's desperate eyes had sought those of the man struggling at the end of a rope for his last breath, the love and heartbreak reflected back at him left no doubt as to who his true father was, blood or no.

That was the exact moment Sully had made the vow of revenge that would change his life forever. And his mother's suicide, moments after her husband's death, only strengthened his determination to make the devil who'd spawned him pay with everything that was dear to his black heart.

Coming back to the present, he took a deep, cleansing breath and physically willed the painful memories away.

Non, he could not, would not, help the boy, Caleb.

But what to do about Elizabeth?

His instincts told him she had no hidden, nefarious purpose to her actions. She only wanted to save her brother by any means possible.

He grimaced, not wanting to believe their incredible night together had been part of those means. *Donc,* if it had been, she had failed. Sleeping with him, regardless of its impact on his heart, would not change his mind.

There was a knock on the door and he swung it open, expecting to see Mrs. Butterfield inquiring about supper. But it was Elizabeth, chin tilted up in challenge, holding his laptop and his stick.

"You left these in my room," she said, and held them out.

Instead of taking the things, he moved to one side. "Come in."

She shook her head. "I don't think—"

"Come *in*," he repeated, more forcefully.

Her spine straightened and she gazed at him defiantly. But she came in. He closed the door and leaned back against it, glancing down at his bad leg.

"Didn't even realize I'd forgotten my stick. Guess the doctor was right about the stairs helping."

"They usually are," she muttered.

She set the offending staff on his bed and wordlessly busied herself with the laptop, plugging in cords and whatnot and flipping open the top. Ignoring him.

He crossed his arms and followed her movements. Graceful, fluid, feminine. She was wearing a delectably short skirt made of blue jeans fabric and one of those tight T-shirts he found so incredibly sexy. Through the thin cloth he could clearly see the outline of her lacy bra. If he looked really hard, would he be able to see the rosy crowns of her breasts?

She turned to him and he tested his theory, unperturbed that she caught him doing it.

He could.

"My offer still stands," she said, her voice even. "Shall I take it off?"

He jerked his gaze up and regarded her. *Far too tempting.* "I would like you to," he admitted, "but it would not further your cause."

Her shapely lips pressed together and she turned away again. "I've set your e-mail to come up automatically when you turn on the laptop. Do you want me to show you how to use it?"

"I would appreciate that."

"Then have a seat."

She'd put the laptop on a dainty pie-edged table, but there was no chair. Silently she pointed to the bed.

"D'accord," he said, and sat down with a grateful sigh. His leg had started to throb again.

"Stop it!" she snapped.

He blinked in surprise. "What?"

She picked up the table, laptop and all, and smacked it down in front of him so hard it rattled. "Stop with the French! You were born in South Carolina, not Louisiana." She put her hands on her hips and glared at him.

"Actually," he said tightly, "I was born in Connecticut, like you."

Her mouth dropped open, and immediately he regretted his rash confession. If she suspected he was lying before, that would clinch it.

"Where?" she demanded. When he didn't answer, her eyes narrowed. "My God, I don't believe it. You *are* after the estate."

When her meaning finally hit home, he vaulted to his feet. *"Non!"* He grabbed for her and staggered, upsetting the table and sending the laptop careening onto the bed. "Is that what you think?"

She jumped back. "Get away from me!" She went for the door and he lunged, whacking it closed as she wrenched it open, and pinning her up against it with his body.

She fought him. She kicked and used her fists, struggling against his superior strength and weight, but she was no match for him, even injured. He could easily have stopped her, but he let her get her blows in. He figured he had it coming. And hopefully hitting him would alleviate some of her anger and frustration over the situation. She needed the outlet.

So she pounded him and he took it, until she was panting and exhausted from the effort, and he was smarting from the walloping.

"You hit like a girl," he ground out when she gave one final thump to his chest and then covered her face with her hands.

She made a tart suggestion that raised his brows. "You want to help me with that?" she asked.

Her fingers slipped down and she peered murderously over them at him. And made the same suggestion, this time tacking on his name.

He gave her a rueful half smile and peeled her hands away from her face. Moisture covered her angry cheeks and glistened from the dark smudges under her eyes. He sighed, and brought her red knuckles to his lips, kissing them one by one.

"*Chère,* whatever you may think of me, know this. I am not after the Sullivan estate or anything like that. I want nothing at all from the Sullivans, and nothing from you that you do not willingly give."

With his thumbs he wiped the salty tears from her face as she searched his.

"I don't understand you," she murmured in soft anguish. "You're a good man under that hard facade. I know you are. Your men worship you, and I…"

"Elizabeth…" he warned. He knew exactly where this was going. Nowhere good.

"He's just a little boy, Sully. Ten years old. Why won't you help him?"

Ten years old. The same age as his sister, he reminded himself harshly, when she was ripped from her dying mother's bloody bosom and sold as an indentured servant to strangers.

He dropped Elizabeth's hands and limped away from her. "I don't want to talk about it," he said through gritted teeth. With difficulty he bent to right the small table and retrieved the laptop from the bed. "Now, show me how to use this blasted contraption."

She didn't want to. He could tell it went against every grain in her body to give in and drop the subject. She undoubtedly felt, in that typically female way, if she could just get him to spill his innermost feelings she could convince him of the error of his ways.

Not this time.

He eased onto the bed and flipped open the laptop, watching as the screen lit up and sprang to life. By the time several pictures had cycled and the machine startled him by greeting him by name, she had come to sit next to him.

"How does it know who I am?" he asked suspiciously.

"I told it," she said, and tersely ran through the basic principles of using the thing. Most of it went right over his head, but he'd always been good with navigation and mechanical devices, so he quickly learned which buttons to push to produce the desired result. Namely to read the several e-mails waiting for him from Tyree, and how to reply to them.

"The spelling is strange," he grumbled. He'd never been a writer—that was Davey Scraggs's domain, along with a few of the more educated men on the crew. Tyree had been a great one for reading and writing. Not Sully. Maps he could read, of course. But he'd rather be tinkering with his ship or mending a sail with the sun on his face than struggling his way through the pages of some esoteric treatise. So he'd never learned the finer points of spelling.

"Don't even try," she said irritatedly, then pointed out a spell check icon and showed him how to use it. "Well, go on. Send him an answer."

Tyree's messages had been short and chatty, giving a few amusing details of their sail through the Bahamas. Inside one was a phone number to contact him ship to shore. In another was a picture of him and Clara waving from the deck of the sleek, modern yacht they were traveling on. Sully smiled, once again astounded by the incredible things that had been invented since his last lifetime. Imagine being able to see someone so clearly from hundreds of miles away. He imagined the phone worked just as well that far, too.

He clicked Reply. And scowled at the keyboard. This was the worst part. It took him several minutes to pick out a greeting and one brief sentence letting his friend know where he was staying.

It didn't help that Elizabeth was sitting right next to him, her warm thigh pressing intimately against his. He could smell the distinctive scent that belonged to only her, sweet and musky all at the same time. He would only have to turn his face and press his nose to her hair, her neck, the shell of her ear, to drink in the full erotic pleasure of her fragrance. How he longed to do so, to surround her with his body and feel her soft curves beneath him one more time.

He felt himself growing hard, and realized his fingers had stalled on the keyboard. When she glanced over at him, his thoughts must have shown clearly on his face, for her eyes suddenly went wide and she started to scoot away.

"Don't," he said, whipping out a hand to halt her. "Stay where you are."

"You can't possibly think—" she began.

With an angry growl, he clicked the send button on his unfinished e-mail and snapped the laptop closed. "What I think is—"

Merde. He shut his mouth before words he'd regret

could spill out. He sighed and snaked an arm around her rigid torso, awkwardly pulling her to his chest. She didn't fight him, but she didn't soften, either. Sliding his fingers into her hair, he pressed his lips to her forehead. He could feel her heart through the layers of their clothes, beating a frantic tattoo as he trailed kisses along her hairline and down her temple, to her cheek, seeking her mouth.

Silently he triumphed. Physically, at least, she still responded to him.

"Sully," she objected, turning away, "this isn't fair."

"And what is?" he murmured philosophically.

She dodged his mouth again. "How can I kiss you when I hate you?"

"But you don't hate me."

"I do."

He tipped up her chin and she looked so miserable he knew it couldn't be further from the truth. "Can we not turn back the clock to yesterday, *chère?* When you wanted me as much as I wanted you?"

"You know that's impossible."

He put his mouth to hers and kissed her gently. "How I wish it weren't."

For a moment she melted against him. She kissed him back, then pulled away, out of his arms. She stood and went to the door, and he didn't have the will to stop her. She gave him a last, sad smile, and then she was gone.

He put his elbows to his knees and gripped his head in his hands. What in blue blazes was he to do? He still wanted her—like crazy he wanted her. And not just for momentary pleasure. In this Elizabeth he recognized a touching depth of soul, of loyalty and…goodness.

Things he had not seen in the Elizabeth of his past—whose easy companionship and come-hither smile had blinded him to the real qualities a woman could offer a man. Ones that mattered.

But it was those very qualities in Elizabeth Hamilton that would keep her from ever accepting him into her life. Because he could not be truthful with her. How could he? How should he tell her what lay in his innermost heart when doing so would reveal an even greater lie? At least she would believe it to be so.

This was an impossible situation.

Why, oh, why had he spoken that damned curse those many years ago? Why had he dared to tamper with God's plan?

And yet, if he hadn't, he would not have come back to life to witness its culmination. Would never have met, nor held in his arms the woman with whom he was falling in love.

Was this his punishment, then? To see the closure of one horrific wound, only to have that very resolution viciously rip open another? Must the scales of cosmic balance always be fed with pain?

With a roar of anger, he flung himself back on the bed.

This would not do! If this lamenting and self-pity continued, he might as well find a good ship and cast himself off its prow into the sea! But that would be a coward's way out. And Sullivan Fouquet may be a lot of things, but a coward was not one of them.

What he needed was a route out of this tangled mess. Some way to avenge his parents, and yet still win the heart of his woman.

Unfortunately, he feared it was hopeless. If there was such a promising solution, the path to it eluded him.

"Nothing?" Elizabeth adjusted her cell phone to her ear and frowned. "You found nothing at all? Are you sure?"

Her mother made an impatient noise. "Not a blessed thing. As far as I can see, there is no feud between the Connecticut and Carolina Sullivans. I just don't understand it."

Elizabeth didn't, either. Although, admittedly, she was having a hard time getting her brain to function. It was late the next morning but she was already on her fifth cup of coffee. Thanks to a completely sleepless night tossing and turning in her feather bed thinking about Sully and his damned contradictions. To no avail, of course. Other than to exasperate herself with the intermittent, unbidden urge to climb the stairs to his room and toss and turn in *his* feather bed. With him.

Oh, Lord.

"Are you listening to me?" her mother demanded.

She fanned herself. "Yes, of course, Mom."

"I stayed up until 2:00 a.m. looking through every book and set of papers I could find, all the way back to the turn of the century. The *last* century! Surely it couldn't have happened before 1900! Who remembers that far back?" Gilda blurted out in frustration.

Elizabeth didn't answer, but mentally flinched. Actually she could think of one person…

Honestly, it was the last thing she really wanted to know, but there was no putting it off.

"Mom, in your research did you happen to run into

anything about Sullivan Fouquet? Some connection to our family?"

She could hear papers rustling. "Yeah. In the household accounts for the mid-to-late 1700s," her mom answered. "Fouquet's name was listed among the servant families. There was a husband, wife and two children who worked on the estate for about thirteen or fourteen years."

"Seventeen-hundreds?" Elizabeth's stomach did a slow roll. The pirate Sullivan Fouquet had died in 1804. The time fit, but… "What happened to them?"

"Doesn't say."

She bit her lip. For some unfathomable reason she was compelled to ask, "So, Sullivan Fouquet, he was the husband?"

There was a pause. She held her breath as more papers rustled.

"No. One of the kids," her mother answered. "The oldest."

Her breath whooshed out in on irrational puff of relief. Though why it should matter, she couldn't fathom.

Lord in heaven, was she ever losing it! Worrying about whether a long-dead pirate had a wife and kids! She already knew Fouquet supposedly had a fiancée after settling in Magnolia Cove. What was so different about a wife? And kids?

And what the heck did it have to do with her, anyway?

Determinedly she shut down the rebellious voice niggling the back of her mind. The one that said it had *everything* to do with her. None of it mattered, in any case. Surely it was a coincidence.

"Why would a servant couple name their kid Sullivan?" she asked grouchily.

"It was a fairly common sign of respect in those days," Gilda explained, "naming a child after the patriarch of the family you worked for. Of course, in this case it was a bit strange…considering."

"Considering what?"

"Oh, didn't I mention? There was a notation after their name in the ledger. The Fouquets were Acadian indentured servants."

Ah, hell. "Acadian?"

"You know. The French Acadians from Nova Scotia. When they were expelled by the British in the 1750s, a lot of them went to Louisiana."

"And became the Cajuns." *So much for coincidence.*

"Exactly. But many stopped here in Connecticut."

Elizabeth managed a noncommittal noise.

"Of course, having been exiled from their homeland and sold into virtual slavery by the British, it's a bit unusual to name a firstborn child in honor of a British lord," Gilda stated.

Elizabeth sucked in a sharp breath as the implications assailed her. "Maybe Lord Henry was nice to them," she choked out.

"Yeah," her mom said, confirming her worst fears, "or maybe he was really, really bad."

"You seem preoccupied. Didn't the physical therapy go well today?"

Sully propped his boots onto Jake's desk with a clunk and gave his friend a wry smile. "You mean the torture? God's Teeth, that woman would have put old Edward Teach to shame." Jake grinned, as Sully knew he would. You couldn't grow up in Magnolia Cove and not know your pirates backward and forward. "But no, it went well enough. She says I'll soon be walking without the cane."

"Already? That's incredible."

"Aye." Sully shrugged unenthusiastically. The sooner he was completely healed, the sooner he'd run out of excuses.

"Then what's bothering you, my friend? Not ready to come back to work yet?"

Jake had an uncanny way of seeing straight to the truth of things. Probably why the man was such a good arson investigator.

When Sully remained silent, uncertain how to answer, Jake tipped his chair onto its back legs and regarded him. "You should think about coming over here to the Magnolia Cove station like I did. It's a lot quieter than Old Fort Mystic. That alarm bell hardly ever rings."

"I'm not a quitter, Jake."

"You'd be transferring. Not quitting. Did I quit when I moved? No."

Sully laced his fingers over his thighs and frowned. "Easy for you to say. You're the department's only arson investigator."

"You'd still be fire chief."

He snorted. "Of a place a tenth the size." It would be like giving up the *Sea Nymph* for command of a river ferry. "I don't want to lose the respect of my men, Jake. I may not remember, but I know the kind of respect they show me was hard-earned. A man has to accept his responsibilities."

"Even if he's not that man anymore?"

Sully's gaze darted to Jake and narrowed. Exactly how much *could* the man see? "What—"

Jake held up his palms. "Down, boy. I only meant that a blind man could see that the fire three months ago changed you. I'm not talking about physically— you'll get over the injuries. I mean in here." He tapped his temple. "And here." He tapped his heart. "This isn't about responsibilities or respect, Andre. It's about what you want out of your life and what you're going to do to get it."

"But—"

"Nobody's going to blame you for reevaluating."

Suddenly an ear-splitting siren blasted through the air. Men started shouting, and downstairs a rumbling engine sprang to life.

Sully's gaze met Jake's in a grim acknowledgment.

No time like the present to face the future.

Chapter 9

There was no hiding from it this time.

The fire was raging by the time the lone fire truck from the Magnolia Cove station made it to the remote island home that had called in the alarm. Ladders from Old Fort Mystic and other stations were on their way, but still over fifteen minutes out. This place was on the edge of the ocean, in the middle of nowhere.

"Forget the bedrooms!" the desperate owner was yelling over the din of men shouting and equipment being unloaded. "Save my office! Oh, my God, three years of work!" he wailed.

Sully had ridden in Jake's smaller yellow truck so the big fire engine could cram in as many volunteer firefighters as possible, scooping them up as they ran out from stores and businesses to meet it as it careened through town. Sully'd been pretty damn impressed by the split-second precision of the maneuvers, every bit as well-executed as any boarding of an enemy vessel he'd orchestrated in his day.

He continued to be impressed as the men tackled their duties upon screeching to a halt in front of the burning structure. Equipment was freed, hoses stretched and water cascading faster than he could figure out how to get his seat belt off.

"The computer!" the owner shouted frantically as two firefighters prevented the man from running back inside the inferno. "Try to get the computer! And the books!"

Smoke and ash swirled thickly all around as Sully eased guardedly from the truck. Immediately the roar of flames filled his ears; his lungs burned from the scorching heat.

"Chief!" Jeremy Swift yelled as Sully fought to quell the instinctive panic. "Grab that shovel and put out those hotspots, okay?"

Jeremy waved at several small patches of flame that had been spit out onto the surrounding dry grass close to the main blaze. Then he was gone.

Desperately Sully glanced around for someone else to do it. But there was no one. Everyone was busy with their own critical task.

His nerves threatened to snap. *Bon Dieu.*

Without giving himself a chance to think, Sully swiped up the shovel, ran over to the hotspots and started pounding them out. They were small. Manageable. Single-mindedly concentrating on his job, he was able to ignore the thundering of his heart and the licking of the huge burning monster behind him and keep the sparks from spreading. With every whack of the shovel, he imagined he was subduing a small piece of his fear. It seemed to work.

At one point someone tossed him a pair of gloves and a helmet with a visor. A bit later Jeremy ran over with a pair of tall rubber boots for him to pull over his shoes and jeans, which were getting so hot he was afraid they might melt any second.

After running around putting out hotspots for what seemed like hours, Sully's arm muscles were screaming with exhaustion, his leg throbbing and his skin burning from the intense heat. But the panic was largely gone.

Needing a breath of fresh air to quell the residual nausea in his stomach, he limped a few yards back into the cooling shade of the junglelike forest that huddled on one side of the property.

And startled a man out of hiding.

"Hey!" Sully shouted as the stranger jumped up from behind a bush and wheeled off, stumbling through the underbrush. "*Arrête!* Stop!"

He took three giant strides after the man, then felt his knee give out. As he started to fall, with an awkward effort he slid the heavy boot off and hurled it at the man. Sully heard a thud and a yell before hitting the ground himself, and rolling to protect his knee.

He was still swearing a blue streak at the stabbing pain when Jake came running up. "What happened?"

He waved a hand after the fleeing man. "There was a guy hiding. Could be involved," he shouted back. "I threw a boot. He might be down. Go!"

Jake took off at a tear. By the time Sully had shaken out his knee and staggered to his feet, Jake came running back. He dropped the boot and a dirty backpack next to Sully and kept right on running.

"Take care of that backpack!" he yelled. "I'm going to cut the bastard off." He jumped in his truck and with a spray of gravel he'd turned it around and was barreling down the road.

Since there was only one bridge onto the tiny coastal island, Sully figured that's where Jake hoped to catch up to the man. He quickly relayed that information to a patrol cop who'd just arrived on the scene, and the cop took off to help.

The fire was under control by this time, its flames nearly battled into submission. But the house was a wreck. Black with soot and sagging under the weight of exposed framework and thousands of gallons of water, it looked as if it would collapse any second. Sully sympathized. He felt the same way.

Hoisting the grimy backpack onto his shoulder, he joined the clutch of firefighters gathered around an engine gulping down water. He was greeted with slaps on the back and a bottle of water thrust into his hand.

"Great job, Chief," several of the guys called. "You'll be back in the swing in a flash!"

"Just like old times!" Jeremy Swift said, grinning widely.

"Got yourself a new cane, boss?" someone said with a chuckle.

Sully looked down and realized he was using the shovel instead of his usual bow-handled walking stick to help him stand. "Well, hell," he muttered. And grinned. Then he started to laugh.

Suddenly he knew he'd be all right. He hadn't been scared, not after banishing the initial panic. He'd done his job and he'd even flushed out the bad guy. His men were now gazing at him with eyes full of respect and affection. He didn't have to say a word. They understood.

And suddenly *he* understood. No matter what choices he made in the future, they'd still respect him.

He'd paid his debt to Andre Sullivan. And now he could let it go—the guilt about being alive and taking over his body. What Sully did with this life from now on was up to him alone.

The question was, what would he do with it? And who would it include…?

Elizabeth and Mrs. Butterfield were drinking afternoon tea—iced sweet tea, of course—in the shade of the veranda when the Magnolia Cove fire engine thundered up to the front gate and from it slid a very tired and sooty figure that Elizabeth could only guess was Sully.

"Oh, my stars!" Mrs. Butterfield declared, dropping her glass and scurrying out to meet him. "Chief Sullivan, what have you been up to?" She flitted around him as he limped up the path—minus his cane, Elizabeth noted—not quite daring to touch his soot-encrusted arms or clothes.

"There was a fire," he said, voice weary, as his eyes met Elizabeth's. "Out on Morrisey Island. Some professor's house."

"Oh, dear!" Mrs. Butterfield said, obviously recognizing the place. "Not Professor Rouse's home? Oh, what a shame! Was he able to save any of his work?"

Sully shook his head, but his gaze never left Elizabeth's. "Don't believe so. Aye, a real shame."

Mrs. Butterfield tutted. "And doubly so because he was almost finished with his book, from what I hear." By this time the pair had reached the front steps and the older woman leaned in conspiratorially, lowering her voice. "Though, perhaps it's an omen. The book was about *voudou,* you know."

Sully and Elizabeth both glanced at her in surprise.

"Voudou?" Sully asked.

Mrs. Butterfield nodded knowingly. "He taught anthropology at the College of Charleston. Was an expert on the Caribbean, and very interested in the old cultural connections between Haiti and South Carolina. Voudou in particular."

Sully staggered, and before Elizabeth knew what she was doing, she had flown down the steps and had her arm around his waist to keep him on his feet. It was a testament to how exhausted he must be that he actually leaned on her.

"Well, it doesn't take a crystal ball to see you need to get inside and lie down," she said worriedly, taking the backpack he had hanging from his shoulder. "Come on. I'll help you upstairs."

"Careful of that backpack," he said, but didn't protest when she urged him up the steps. "It might be evidence."

"Was the fire bad?" she asked.

"Bad enough."

"Were you…okay?"

They stopped in the foyer to gather themselves for the climb upstairs. He looked down at her and smiled. "Just fine."

Despite the thousand conflicting emotions triggered within her by that smile, she returned it. His refusal to help her brother would always paint her feelings for Sully with the brush of anguish, but…she couldn't deny the feelings were there. Their mutual attraction practically lit up the room with the sparks it generated. And if he were any other man in any other circumstances, she would be falling even harder for him. She didn't know what it was, but there was something about Andre Sullivan that had toppled her defenses and crept into her heart. By all rights she should hate him, or at least resent him. But the truth was, she adored him.

Maybe it was the sexy way he looked at her with those sultry bedroom eyes, or the confident way he touched her with his gentle, powerful hands. Or his sculpted mouth, so firm and skillful…

"I'm getting soot all over you," he murmured, trailing a finger over her cheek, and she realized she was just standing there staring up at him. Probably with her heart pinned to her sleeve for anyone to see.

"Don't worry about it," she said, shaking off the impossible longing and attempting to get businesslike. Armed with her mom's new information, maybe the test situation was still salvageable. "But you better clean up before lying down on Mrs. B's pretty lace duvet. You're a mess."

"Here you are," Mrs. Butterfield sang out, hurrying up to them with a bright pink box. "Bubble bath! I just knew I had some tucked away. Turn on the jets, and have a nice, soothing soak."

"Jets? You have a spa tub?" Elizabeth demanded of Sully, mocking affront.

"Doesn't everyone?" he asked with a grin.

"No fair."

"I got spoiled in physical therapy." He winked. "I'll share this one with you."

It took them a while to make it all the way up, first halting on the second-floor landing for a lively debate. Sully wanted to stop at her room. She held out for the spa tub. She could see he needed those jets.

Plus, she had a sinking feeling she knew exactly what would happen if he stayed in her room again. She might be mad as hell at him, but her body still vividly recalled what it was like to lie under him, feeling the full power of his attentions. Resisting that would be next to impossible.

They continued to the third floor.

The massive spa tub was raised up in front of a multipaned bow window overlooking the tree-dotted meadow that led down to a tide inlet behind the Inn. In the muted tones of late afternoon, the view was gorgeous, like something out of a Monet landscape. The scent of vanilla and cinnamon candles wafted up from the tub surround, and the cheerful chirping of birds in the trees sifted in through an open casement window, completing the atmosphere of cozy luxury.

"This'll feel great on your tired muscles," she said, turning on the taps for him. "But you should probably soap off the worst grime before filling the tub."

"Stay," he said softly, putting his hand on her arm when she turned to go. "I may need help."

"Sully…"

"It's not like you haven't seen me naked before," he reasoned with a tempting smile.

She hesitated just long enough for it to be her undoing.

"I promise to be good," he said, peeling off his grubby T-shirt. "Hmm, I should probably just throw this away, *non?*"

He looked like a coal miner, the black soot standing out in stark contrast to his lighter skin, but it matched the masculine thatch of hair on his chest, which trailed down to—the pants he was unzipping! She let out a small gasp, whirling around to whip open the large plastic bag Mrs. Butterfield had given her along with the bubble bath.

"Here," he said.

Before she could stop him he'd walked around her and dumped his soiled clothes into the bag.

He was stark naked. And even with dirt and grime covering a good portion of it, his body was tempting as hell.

Oh, Lord.

"How do I get in?" he asked.

She blinked.

"That monstrosity," he clarified, pointing at the tub.

She felt her face go warm. "Oh. Um, just climb over the side."

He turned to her and hiked a brow. "A hand, perhaps?"

She licked her lips, told herself she was being a ninny and went to help.

This was ridiculous. The man only wanted a bath, for crying out loud.

Yeah, right. Did they sell swampland in South Carolina?

Going up the raised platform wasn't bad, but his knee protested the steep drop down into the tub. She was forced to kick off her sandals and go first, catching him around his waist—his *naked* waist—as he stepped over.

Somehow she ended up in his arms. His *naked* arms. They wrapped around her and held on.

"I thought you were going to be good," she said primly, her pulse nevertheless taking off into hyperspace.

"Just getting my balance," he murmured, warm water swirling around their feet. And knocked her off hers even more by putting his lips to hers.

The kiss was short but intense. His tongue swept into her mouth, plundered, then receded, his teeth giving her lower lip a tiny nip as he lifted up. He didn't protest when she disentangled herself and scrambled out of the tub, sucking at the tiny sting he'd left on her lip.

"What was that for?"

He picked up the business end of the six-foot shower hose and fiddled with the tap lever. "To make you think of me."

For some primitive, irrational reason, his low-spoken declaration shot through her center, a flash of hot desire.

A burst of water spurted onto him and immediately rivulets of black started to run down his body. She watched with heated, unwilling fascination as he moved the shower spray over his torso and limbs, black turning to gray, then fading into olive skin scored with intermittent lines and patches of angry red as he scrubbed. Even with the scars from his accident, he was magnificent. Lean and muscular, broad-shouldered and oh, so—

"There's no soap," he said, jerking her attention up from…places it had no business being.

With burning cheeks, she scanned the tub surround. "Here." She bent to retrieve a pretty turquoise seashell-shaped designer soap from an oyster shell dish.

He made an incredulous face. "That's soap?"

"You doubt me?"

He leveled her a gaze containing a hint of challenge. "Maybe. Why don't you prove it?"

Their eyes met and suddenly she was hard-pressed to remember her name, much less why she shouldn't strip off her clothes and accept his dare.

His half-lidded gaze beckoned her to sin, tempted her to forget about the million complications existing between them, and the million more this would engender. Wooed her to accept the blissful pleasure she knew he would gift her with if she gave in.

What would it hurt? she rationalized. Already knowing her mind was made up. They'd slept together once before. And growing even closer to him could only soften his attitude to her cause—the reason she'd shied away from getting involved with him in the first place. But at this point, she'd abandoned any pretense of fairness or ethics concerning Caleb's welfare.

She'd also abandoned any delusions regarding her shameless desire for the man in front of her.

She wanted him.

Beyond all reason, she wanted him.

"I won't give up," she said stubbornly. He had to know where she stood.

"I can't give in," he returned, his eyes boring holes through her.

"All's fair in love and war," she stated in warning. That she would use any means to win.

His cruel mouth softened, curved sensually. "Ah, welcome to my world, *mon amour.*"

The world of a pirate, she thought suddenly, irrationally.

Then shoved that thought aside. His insidious pheromones must be sabotaging her grasp on reality as well as her good sense. The man did *not* come from the eighteenth century!

But whether he did or didn't made little difference in his very male reaction when she unzipped her sundress and let it slither down her hips. It was instant and unambiguous.

Her heartbeat thundered as he slowly took in every inch of her, from her toes to her nose and everything in between.

Mostly everything in between.

She had made a short trip to the village yesterday morning while he was at physical therapy—back before the spit had hit the fan about the whole Sullivan thing—to a small, exclusive boutique she'd spotted earlier. Called Sweet Secrets Lingerie.

Apparently he approved of her purchases.

He swallowed heavily, watching her with predatory eyes as she stepped into the tub. But he didn't touch her.

"I'm still covered in grime," he said, low and gravelly. "Come one step closer and you will be, too."

She tilted her head seductively. And held up the soap. "We'll see about that, won't we? Now, turn around."

Sully groaned softly when Elizabeth took the shower nozzle from him and pushed on his shoulder with a single finger. Though it was the last thing he wanted to do, he presented her with his back.

He thought briefly about the burns and scars that now marred his body. Thank God she didn't seem to mind them, spraying him and gliding the silly little soap over his skin until the lather flowed white. Was that a soft kiss he felt on his newly mended shoulder blade?

Her hands and fingers were like heaven on his weary flesh, massaging and coaxing life into body parts that an hour ago had seemed all but dead. Very soon he was anything but tired.

"Sit down," she ordered, when she had set every inch of his skin blazing with her sweet, soapy touch. She looked so provocative wearing those two tiny bits of transparent blue lace…and ordering him around. Did she not realize *he* was the captain here?

He quirked up the corner of his lip. She'd see soon enough who was in command when she surrendered to him. Under him.

For now he decided to indulge her. He sat.

She flipped a lever and water started pouring from the taps. Then she added powder from Mrs. Butterfield's pink box. It smelled like flowers. And the tub was filling with masses of white foam bubbles.

He frowned. "I won't be able to see you."

"Sight can be overrated," she said, returning from across the room where she'd gone to fetch one of the small packets that had been among Tyree's going-away survival kit.

"That's a matter of opinion," he murmured as she slid off her panties and joined him. When she reached for her bra, he stopped her. "Leave it on." Women's underthings these days were so different…erotic as hell. Seeing Elizabeth's lush curves shown off in that gossamer bit of froth made his head spin and his arousal rampant.

She gave him a sexy little smile. "Tell me if I hurt you," she said, and climbed onto his lap.

"You're kidding, right?"

He pulled her to him and savored the feel of her breasts as they pillowed into his chest, round and perfect and calling to his mouth to explore them, and her thighs, which slid over his, pressing their lower bodies together intimately. He wanted to lift and impale her. Make her his completely, claim her body as his personal property and dominion of pleasure. Even in his days as a pirate he'd never wanted anything so painfully and exquisitely as he wanted Elizabeth Hamilton to be his. His alone.

"I want you, too," she murmured. *Had he spoken aloud?* "Oh, Andre, I want you, too."

The name jerked him from his sexual haze. "Not Andre," he growled. "*Never* call me Andre."

Her gaze flew up to his. And filled with something indefinable. "All right, how's this?" she murmured, wrapping her arms about his neck and her knees about his waist. She brushed a kiss over his cheekbone and whispered in his ear, "I want you, too…Sullivan Fouquet."

Chapter 10

Sully froze.

"What are you saying?" he asked, his voice a barely audible grate against the running water. He didn't dare to hope the implication was as it seemed—a sentiment so profound, and unexpected, he was taken aback.

Her hands slipped down to toy with the hair on his chest. "You believe you're Sullivan Fouquet," she said—not a question, he noted—and pressed a lingering kiss to his jaw. "I can work with that."

She touched his nipples and he nearly lost his train of thought. "But *you* don't believe it," he retorted.

"Sully, do we have to talk about this now?" she murmured, raking her fingernails down his torso.

"Aye." He seized her wrists in one hand and

wrenched off the faucets with the other. The sudden silence was deafening. "We do."

She nestled closer in his lap. The resulting wave of iridescent bubbles left a trail of suds clinging to the upper swell of her breasts. His lust took a further upswing, but he wouldn't let it distract him.

"All right, fine," she said with a sigh. "Those trick memories you say you have... Do you remember *everything?* About Sullivan Fouquet's life, I mean. Or just bits and pieces?"

"Does it matter?"

"Yes, because if you do remember everything, it would explain...certain things...that otherwise make no sense."

"Such as?"

"Do we *really* have to get into this now?" She undulated against him. "I can think of better games than twenty questions."

So could he, but *after.*

She slanted him a glance from under her lashes, and tugged at her captured wrists. "Especially if you really are a pirate..."

His jaw dropped and he teetered on the razor's edge of temptation. Elizabeth Hayden had enjoyed that game, too. Pirate and captive. *Sacre—*

He whisked her wrists behind her back and held her firmly between his arms, so she couldn't squirm. She gazed up at him, her smooth skin flushed with excitement, the pretty peaks of her breasts like hard little pebbles against him.

Slowly, agonizingly slowly, he lifted her, adjusted, then let her glide, inch by torturous inch, onto him. He watched her sky-blue eyes darken to indigo as he filled her. Her mouth leaned forward, seeking his, but he held his lips just out of reach.

"Sully," she whispered. "You're killing me here."

"Do you believe, Elizabeth?" he murmured. "Do you believe in the impossible?"

Indigo eyes turned pleading. "I'm not sure."

"Who am I, Elizabeth?" he softly demanded. "Who?"

"I—I honestly don't know," she said, her expression going desperate.

"Who is the man you've let inside you, Elizabeth? What's my name?" He was torturing her, but he had to know where he stood.

"You're Sully."

He brought her up, up to the throbbing tip of him, and let her down again. She whimpered. "But which Sully?"

"I don't know! Please—"

He narrowed his eyes at her. *"Which one, Lizzie?"*

"You really are Sullivan Fouquet, aren't you…?" It came out in hushed tones of awe-filled resignation. And for a moment his heart stopped beating. "I don't know how," she said, "or why, but somehow…you've come back, haven't you?"

He couldn't draw breath, and felt himself in imminent danger of perishing from shock and empty lungs. "You truly believe that?" he asked, managing to keep his voice relatively even.

"It's impossible," she murmured. "And yet, here you are, alive. Inside me."

He let her wrists go then, and they came together in a fierce hug. *"Mon coeur,"* he murmured, unable to credit what was happening. He didn't know what to say, how to thank her in words for her belief in him— in the miracle of his existence.

So he showed her in the next best way, with his body. And for the first time in his life—either life—he understood what it was to make love. First almost desperately in the luxurious tub, a savage claiming that sent water and bubbles splashing everywhere. Then in his bed— this time a slow, intense joining of flesh and spirit that left him reeling with emotions he'd never before experienced.

He'd wanted Elizabeth from the first moment he'd seen her. First in mistaken identity, but then for herself, the woman he came to realize was far superior in every way. But even in his admiration and growing attachment, his craving for her was like those of his pirate days, to claim her as a prize, to own her and call her his. A beautiful treasure to be enjoyed in private and shown off in public.

But now...now his feelings ran fathoms, oceans, deeper. Could this be love? *Real* love—not infatuation or possessiveness, but the kind of love that turned a man inside out and shook him to his very soul? The kind that could make a man reevaluate his life and everything he'd always *believed* to be real? He'd never experienced that kind of love before. But he was beginning to think this could be it.

As he lay there with his woman in his arms, the glow of a new day dawning over the windowsill, he couldn't help thinking about those things he'd always held sacred in his life above all others. Duty. Honor. Revenge.

He'd never thought love for a woman would affect any of those things. One had nothing to do with the other. But Elizabeth Hamilton changed all that. What good was honor if it wasn't given to the woman you loved? And duty—duty to family, or duty to her? But the worst was revenge. To have one, he must surely give up the other.

But how could he choose? *Le Bon Dieu,* how the hell could he ever choose?

Elizabeth woke to the unfamiliar, but wickedly wonderful feeling of a man settling between her thighs and coming into her.

Sully.

"Mmm," she hummed, and wrapped her arms around him as he blissfully joined their bodies. Any awkwardness that might have arisen because of the mind-blowing intensity of the previous night vanished in the joy of being one again. It had not been a quirk or a fluke, it really did feel this good being together.

And when it was over and he lingered on top of her, giving her kisses and drawing lazy circles on her naked skin, she wished they could stay like this forever. That the world wouldn't intrude on their perfect union with its conflicts and deadly diseases and laws of scientific impossibilities.

"You look so serious," he said quietly. "What are you thinking about, *mon amour?*"

She sent him a smile she hoped covered her inner uncertainties. Should she give him platitudes, or the truth?

Neither were right for the moment, so she just gave

him a kiss instead. "I'm thinking how much I don't want to get out of bed."

His expressive lips curved up. "Then let's don't. We can stay here all day. After overdoing it so badly at the fire yesterday, I'm sure my doctor will approve a day of rest."

She raised a coquettish eyebrow. "Rest? In that case, never mind."

He grinned. "You are being a very bad girl, Elizabeth Hamilton."

"Only recently," she assured him with a kiss. "After getting involved with a very bad boy."

"The kind your mother always warned you about?" he teased.

She made a face. "Actually she encouraged me to stick with you. Of course, I didn't mention the pirate thing…."

Above her, Sully tensed. "You told your mother about me?"

"I tell my mother everything. Well—" she gave a rueful grimace "—nearly everything."

"So Gilda Sullivan knows…about us? Our relationship?"

"Afraid so. Minus the reincarnation stuff. The situation seemed complicated enough without tossing that into the mix."

"Transmigration," he corrected, rolled off her and jetted out a breath, covering his eyes with his hands. Then he said something in French it was probably just as well she couldn't understand. "Caleb Sullivan knows about me, too?"

She nodded. "The G-rated version. Is there a problem, Sully?"

"What the hell do you think?"

And just like that, the magic of the night was wiped away, replaced by the irresolvable differences that hovered ever-present between them.

She swallowed, and touched him, the man who had brought her so much pleasure, and for a few hours made her feel like the only woman in the world.

"Sully, please… Isn't there some way—"

"Non!" he cut her off harshly, then backpedaled and said more gently, "I'm sorry, but you know where I stand on helping the Sullivans."

Her heartbeat skittered. Now would be the time to bring it up—the information her mother had uncovered. And the suspicions it had raised in Elizabeth's mind, about the origins of his animosity.

She gathered her courage, and asked, "Because of Lord Henry?"

He bolted upright on the bed and rounded on her. "What do you know of Lord Henry?" he demanded.

She sat up, too, and pulled the sheet around her. "Mom found some old records in the estate archives, from his time. There was reference to a Fouquet family. Servants."

"And?"

"And my mother surmised from his name that the son, Sullivan, had been… That is, that Lord Henry was his—your?—real father."

Sully looked as though she'd slapped him. He reeled from the bed and paced unevenly away from it. Staring through the window, he ground out, "Your mother is a very perceptive woman. However, I can assure you of one thing. Lord Henry may have sired me, but he was in no way my father."

The roughly spoken pronouncement sent goose bumps searing down Elizabeth's flesh. This was not the voice of a man suffering from delusions. It was the voice of a man suffering from injustice. *Personal* injustice.

A wave of unreality hit her—from the certain knowledge that she was falling in love with— What? A ghost? A demon? What had he said, transmigration? Lord, a *body-snatcher?*

She smothered an hysterical laugh. Good Lord.

"Elizabeth, I know what you must be thinking."

"I doubt it," she muttered, rubbing the goose bumps from her arms.

He glanced at her sharply. "I'm sorry if you find my motives amusing or inadequate—"

"No. It's not that."

"What, then?"

"It's either laugh…or cry." She pushed out a long sigh and flopped back on the pillow. "The whole situation is so bizarre. I keep thinking any minute now I'll wake up and this will all have been just a terrible—" she sent him a heartfelt glance "—wonderful, awful dream."

The anger in his face drained away, leaving just the stark tension. He came to sit on the edge of the mattress and took her hand, lacing his fingers through hers. "Elizabeth, these past three months have been a nightmare for me. Being in the hospital, my body a wreck. Not knowing for certain who I really am, why I'm here, or what forces were at work to bring me back from…wherever I was before. It wasn't until I met you that I felt the least inkling of…comfort. Or of belonging."

God, she didn't want to hear this. Didn't want to know of his misery, his vulnerability. It would only make what she had to do even harder. "Sully—"

"*Non,* let me finish. I want you to stay with me, *chère.* Move down here to Magnolia Cove and—"

"Stop!" she exclaimed, yanking her hand from his and jumping from the bed they'd shared. She stared at him incredulously. "I can't believe you can ask me that, and in the next breath refuse to help my brother!"

"I'd hoped—"

"Well, don't. Despite everything, I like you, Sully. God help me, I more than like you. But don't offer me something you know I can never accept. It's too cruel."

With that she swiped up her dress from the floor, pulled it on and rushed out the door before he could catch her.

"Elizabeth!" he yelled after her.

But she didn't want to listen. Anything he had to say would only make the hurt worse.

This was so unfair. So goddamned unfair! Why did she have to fall for a man she could never have?

Stubborn, stubborn male pride! Poor Caleb had nothing to do with long-dead Lord Henry Sullivan. And if Sully couldn't see that, he wasn't the kind of man she wanted in her life.

No matter how much her heart and body disagreed.

Watching Elizabeth flee, for the first time in his life Sully was hit with an overwhelming sense of helplessness. Not even as they'd tied him behind a horse and dragged him from his weeping sister and the dead bodies of his parents, away from the Sullivan estate to be transported to Louisiana, had he felt this unsure of himself. Back then he'd had a powerful purpose. One that had carried him through a difficult youth and forged him into the iron-willed man he'd become. The man he was even today.

But had that iron will begun to rust and weld fast to itself, in the shape of an outdated and unnecessary need for revenge?

He scrubbed his face to banish the mental images that awful day conjured for him. Horrific, sickening images of his family slain, his heart torn apart.

Non! Someone had to pay for that destruction! For that loss of potential and innocence. He *must* stay the course. Elizabeth didn't understand. How could she, when she didn't have the whole story? But would she listen if he told her?

Would it help?

Probably not. She loved her brother. No excuse would be good enough to trump that love. And to be honest, he did not begrudge her. Loyalty was a trait he admired, even when it went against his interests.

So there it was again. The impasse that tore at them and their love like a savage hurricane splintering a ship to pieces.

What was there to do about it? Short of tying her to his bed for the rest of their lives, he could think of nothing.

His gaze fell to the bathroom floor where the water still pooled, a reminder of the passion they both found impossible to ignore. How could he simply stand aside and allow a passion like that to die? Or more likely, survive for a lifetime of loneliness, doomed by vicious circumstance not to flourish?

As he washed and dressed for his morning physical therapy appointment, he imagined himself back on the quarterdeck of the *Sea Nymph,* puzzling out how to penetrate an impenetrable harbor defense, or defeat an undefeated enemy admiral. Those challenges had never posed a problem for him in the past. This one, too, surely had a solution, if he could but see it.

In the meantime, the first rule of capture was not to let the prize out of your sight. He must keep Elizabeth close. Keep her talking to him. If possible, keep making love to her. And perhaps even, against all his instincts, hope for Caleb to make a miraculous recovery…without Sully's help.

Elizabeth put the receiver back down onto the phone in her room, feeling worried.

It had been a call from her mother, telling her Caleb had taken a small turn for the worse overnight.

The night Elizabeth had spent making love to his sworn enemy.

A cry escaped her, and she put her hand over her mouth to prevent more from following. *Enemy.* How could a ten-year-old boy be *anyone's* enemy? It was absurd!

Her mom had assured her Caleb was okay, just not feeling as well as he had been. But any change in his condition worried Elizabeth. What if he got even worse? What if he had to go back into the hospital and she wasn't there? What if she really couldn't talk Sully into doing the test? What if—

Oh, God. She had to do something!

A knock sounded on her door and she went to answer it, swiping a tear from her lashes.

Think of the devil and he appeared. It was Sully.

One thing you had to say for the man, he had the audacity of a fox and the stubbornness of a mule. Too bad those things were working against her and not with her.

"Are you all right?" he asked with a frown.

She took a deep breath and nodded.

He looked dubious, but said, "You're obviously still not speaking to me," he said with a shade of contrition, "but I was hoping you might drive me to my physio this morning. You don't need to say anything," he added when she remained mute, needing a minute to gather herself and switch gears. "Just nod."

She sighed. "Honestly, Sully. I'm not a petulant child."

"Non," he agreed. "So, how about it? We can have breakfast first. I, for one, built up quite an appetite last night."

She snapped him a look, but his expression was perfectly neutral.

"I got a call from my mom," she said as they descended the stairs, not wanting to talk about last night. "Caleb isn't feeling well."

He paused in taking a step. "I'm sorry." The sentiment actually seemed sincere. "It must be difficult for you. Especially being so far away."

"I'm thinking of flying home."

"Non!" They'd reached the bottom of the stairway,

and he swung to grasp her arms, spinning her to face him. "Don't go yet. Please."

"Why?" she asked. "He needs me. Unless...are you telling me you might still change your mind and have the test?"

His fingers dug into her flesh. "*Non.* You know that's not possible."

"Then what reason would I have for staying?" she demanded, guilt instantly flooding over her when his gaze flinched with hurt.

"For me. Because *I* need you."

He was doing his best to pull her strings, and the worst part was, he was succeeding. She couldn't *do* this. "You're a real bastard, Sully."

He gave a humorless laugh. "You don't know the half of it, *chère.*"

"So tell me."

His eyes drilled into hers. "I will, if you stay."

She wasn't sure she trusted him this far. He had his own agenda, and keeping her was apparently part of it. Not that it wasn't flattering, in a very basic, primitive way. But she would not be swayed against her better judgment.

Still, if there was more to his reasons that she didn't know, she wanted to hear it. You couldn't fight what you didn't know.

"Promise?" she asked.

"I swear." The grandfather clock in the foyer chimed nine, breaking the tension crackling between them. "But I'll be late if we don't get moving now. *Vien.*"

After a quick breakfast, she drove him to the medical center then sat in the waiting room as he did his physical therapy. On the chair next to her he'd left the backpack he'd carried home with him last night from the scene of the fire. He said he didn't want to leave it in the car in case it got stolen. On the phone Jake had said it might be evidence, and asked if they could peek in and tell him what was there.

Evidence of what?

Curious, she unzipped the top a few inches and peered inside. The backpack was filled with what appeared to be old books. Hmm.

She recalled the conversation she and Sully'd had with Mrs. Butterfield over dinner a few days ago, where their hostess had said the arsonist plaguing the area was supposedly after some two-hundred-year-old paintings, and diaries written by a sailor. Specifically, diaries that had to do with a voudou curse placed on someone by—

Oh, my God!

Sullivan Fouquet!

How could she have forgotten that?

What was more, hadn't Mrs. Butterfield said that yesterday's arson victim was a professor who specialized in voudou?

Once again a sense of unreality washed over Elizabeth. Sullivan Fouquet's sudden reappearance—if she really believed that—could it have something to do with…*voudou?*

Normally Elizabeth was a fairly practical person. Not given to flights of fancy. Heck, she didn't even read her horoscope—she thought the whole thing was a lot of hooey. Ghosts? Well, maybe. The universe, after all, was a miraculous, mysterious place, and who was Elizabeth Hamilton to set limits to its powers?

But voudou?

Good grief. Was any of this really possible?

A long shiver traced itself up her spine and down again.

Perhaps she should just take a little peek *inside* the diaries. See what she could find out. She'd be very careful. Only touch the edges. Maybe— What was the arsonist's name? Wes? Wesley Orange? Pulp? Peel! That was it—maybe Wesley Peel had found and marked the passage he'd been seeking in the journals. The one about the curse.

Maybe that could shed some light on, or give her some insight into what drove the man, Sullivan Fouquet.

Knowing she'd probably regret it, but unable to help herself, Elizabeth pulled the top diary from the backpack and began to read.

Chapter 11

"What the hell?"

Elizabeth looked up in surprise, then guiltily shut the sailor's diary she'd been thoroughly engrossed in for the past half hour. "Sully!"

"Where did you get those?" he demanded, scanning the volume in her hands as well as those stacked on the chair beside her.

"Um. The backpack, I'm sorry. I know I probably shouldn't have touched them, but when I saw what they were I just couldn't resist. And Jake did say to find out…"

"God's Bones, those are Davey Scraggs's journals! How on earth did they get—" His eyes widened and he plopped down in the plastic chair on the other side of the diaries. "So it *was* Wesley Peel at the fire. He dropped the backpack when Jake started chasing him." Sully reached out to pick one up, but his hand stopped and hovered above it, almost as though he was afraid to touch it.

"Fascinating reading," she ventured, watching him carefully.

His gaze snapped to hers. "Oh, aye?"

She nodded. Waiting.

The corner of his lip curled up wryly. "You mean to assess my knowledge, don't you?"

Her face went warm that her intent was so transparent. But this was an opportunity that would only come once, and she wouldn't back down. "If you really are Fouquet…"

"Are you certain you want to know the truth?"

"You're that sure?"

"Trust me, there is nothing in those diaries I can't tell you about in greater detail than is written here. At least—" he shrugged "—the ones penned before my death."

Another shiver sifted through her. *Did* she want to know the truth? Well, didn't she already believe, in her heart of hearts, that however improbable, this man really was Sullivan Fouquet?

Or was it that the alternative would be too awful to bear—that Andre Sullivan was a complete fraud…about everything from feigning amnesia to his reasons for not being tested for Caleb? And their affair—it would make that a sham, too, and her a gullible idiot for believing something so preposterous.

"Would you object?" she asked.

"I'll welcome it if it means putting to rest any doubts you have about me."

"Well, I wouldn't go that far," she said, but managed a smile when his brow rose.

He made a face. "Let's get out of here. If I must endure an inquisition, I'd like to be somewhere more comfortable, and preferably with a glass of ale in my hand."

"But shouldn't we get the backpack to Jake first?"

"I called him from the nurse's station to ask about it. He said to hang on to it for now. Apparently Peel slipped past them yesterday, and he's working another lead to catch him."

"That's great. I'd like to read more."

"Before or after my inquisition?"

She chuckled. "I saw a jetty out behind Pirate's Rest. How about we go there and talk? We could pick up a six-pack."

"Perfect."

First they stopped at the Inn to change. While Sully continued up to his room, Elizabeth dug through her suitcase for her bikini and a pair of shorts. She was just getting out the sunblock when he reappeared in her doorway. Looking much as before. He'd only switched his polo shirt for a T-shirt.

"Aren't you wearing shorts?" she asked, examining his attire critically. "It's hot out there."

"Shorts?" He tore his gaze from her bikini top and glanced down at himself uncertainly.

It took a bit of convincing, but ten minutes later, kicking and screaming the whole time, he'd changed into navy gym shorts, a white sleeveless T-shirt and an

Old Fort Mystic FD baseball cap that she scrounged from the dresser in his room. She pulled on her own UConn ball cap and headed for the door.

"You are not going out like *that?*" he asked, exchanging horror over his own attire for hers—or rather her lack of it.

"We're just walking down to the water. No big deal."

"But people will see you!"

"It's a bathing suit, Sully. That's what women wear to the beach these days."

"Not *my* woman!" he declared with a scowl.

There were so many possible reactions to that vehement statement—the thrill of being claimed so adamantly as his, irritation at the chauvinist edict of what she could and couldn't wear, despair at having to deny the relationship he so patently envisioned they were in—all she could do was stare.

Rather than deal with all that, she wordlessly went back into her room and pulled a light camp shirt on over her bikini top.

"Better?"

Something of the war waging tightly within her must have shown on her face, because his shoulders notched down and he said, "Some things take a man longer to get used to. Sharing your body with the world—" He shook his head. "Not there yet."

"Don't worry about it."

"Bad enough I have to share my own," he muttered with a scowl at his bare legs, and followed her down the stairs.

Inwardly, she gave in to a half smile. Okay. She supposed her covering up was a fair trade for making him change into those sexy shorts. With any luck both their shirts would be off before the afternoon was out and he'd be over his prudish attitude toward bathing attire.

As for the rest…well, that remained to be seen.

The day was hot, but absolutely glorious.

The narrow wooden jetty behind the Inn stretched at least a hundred feet out into the sparkling inlet, past the shallows where the spartina and sea oats swayed near the shore and out into deeper water where you could tie up a boat or do some fishing if you were so inclined.

A cool breeze blew up the narrows from the open ocean beyond a collection of smaller islands that crowded around Frenchman's Island. Mrs. Butterfield had packed a picnic basket with lunch and lent them a couple of beach towels to sit on, so they'd spread it all out and cracked open the six-pack, and were now lying contentedly on their backs watching the pelicans play dive-bomber.

"*Dieu!* How I miss the sea," Sully said with a frustrated sigh.

Elizabeth rolled to her side and propped an elbow on the rough wooden decking, cradling her head in her hand. "Tell me about being a pirate," she urged, wanting nothing more than to listen to his deep, melodious voice sharing tales of the life he'd had before she was born. Hell, before her great-grandmother was born.

"Privateer," he corrected with a sardonic smile. "Remember?"

"Right. But weren't you a pirate first?"

"Aye, though we confined ourselves to enemy vessels, even before gaining our letters of marque. Except for the slavers, of course. They were always fair game in my eyes, regardless of origin."

So she'd gathered, from reading through a couple of the diaries while waiting at the hospital. Davey Scraggs had spared no detail in telling of the several merchant vessels the *Sea Nymph* had boarded and taken during the two years those particular journals chronicled. He'd also reminisced richly about the "old days" in between those colorful descriptions, as well as going on about the abominably heartbreaking conditions on the one or two slavers they'd liberated, too.

"You were a good captain," she said, using Scraggs's oft-repeated assessment of Sully's abilities. "The men liked you."

"Aye," he agreed softly. "A leader is always better for having labored at the bottom of the chain himself."

She wanted desperately to hear about those times, when he'd worked as a servant boy on the vast Sullivan estates of the 1700s. But sensed he wasn't there yet, either. "Tell me about taking the merchantman in '96," she said, settling back down for a good story. The entry in Scraggs's journal had made her laugh out loud—parts of it, anyway.

Sully grinned. "Ah, the *Maria Estrella Encantada.* Now that was a fun one," he said, obviously knowing exactly to which adventure she was referring. "Her hold was full of good Cuban rum, the passenger cabins over-flowing with lovely aristocratic Spanish *señoritas* being sent back to the old country as bartered brides and the captain's quarters fairly sizzled from the vivacious presence of the captain's wild Irish mistress."

Elizabeth already knew who ended up with the exotic but incorrigible Irishwoman—Captain Tyree St. James of the *Sea Nymph*'s sister ship and constant companion, the *Sea Sprite*—or she would never have brought up the subject.

"Those poor innocent Spanish *señoritas*," she observed with a disapproving frown. The one thing that had given her pause about the incident. "Being thrown to a pack of savage pirates—er, *privateers*." Such scenarios might be the stuff of spicy romance novels, but the reality of it she was sure had been far from romantic.

Sully snorted eloquently. "Innocent? Ha!" Then his eyes lost all trace of humor, narrowing dangerously. "And you do realize, don't you, that rape was a hanging offense even on pirate vessels? Strictly against the Code."

"No," she said, surprised, especially by his sudden turn in mood. "I had no idea."

"*Alors,* there may have been exceptions," he said with thick intensity, "but my ship was assuredly not among them." Then, just as suddenly, his smile returned. "*Non,* those *señoritas,* they were smart, headstrong girls bound for lives of closeted servitude under the yokes of crusty old noblemen they'd never even met, in a country they'd never lived in. They were used to the relative freedom of the Caribbean colonies, and most resented having to give it up. Can you blame some of them for choosing to take their fates into their own hands?" He grinned and gave her a wink. "But not without some lively bartering first."

Well, that didn't sound so bad. She was possibly being delusional, but she believed him. As captain he no doubt had protected those girls and any other innocents who'd landed under his care during his life as a brigand, legal or no. His reaction just now said it all; his honor would let him do no less.

He continued the tale, filling in where Davey Scraggs had left off, and then went on to regale her with a dozen more adventures, each more entertaining than the last. Each liberally spiced with gold and jewels, liquor and women of easy virtue. The latter, he was always careful to point out—as had Scraggs—inevitably ending up in St. James's bed, usually much to the other captain's misadventure and the amusement of the crews.

"And what about you, Sully?" she asked as he chuckled at another of Tyree's romantic foibles. "All those women…"

"Ah, *chère*. If you've read a single entry in those diaries, you'll know I was ever-faithful to your namesake." The laughter faded and again his expression clouded. "And more the fool for it."

She turned to him. "What did she do?"

"It seems she plotted behind my back to relieve me of my wealth. Using my love for her as a weapon against me." He took a long swig of beer. "The signs were all there. I was just too blinded by her allure to see them."

Elizabeth turned away again, all of a sudden uncomfortable. Was she doing the same thing? If you substituted "wealth" for "bone marrow"…?

"Don't worry, *chère*," he said, as if sensing her guilt trip. "You have been honest with me about your plotting. If she had been as honest, had she but asked me, I would have given her everything she desired…."

And yet Elizabeth had asked him over and over for what *she* needed, only to be refused each time. Sorely piqued, she sat up and wrenched off the top of another beer. "How nice for her," she muttered under her breath.

She didn't know what it was, the thought of him loving another woman so much he'd give up everything for her, or his continuous flat refusal to help her brother, or the reality-bending fact of his present existence, or a combination of it all. Or hell, maybe just too much sun. But whatever it was, she suddenly couldn't take any more.

He'd proven without a doubt who he was. But she was in no mood to press him about the subject she'd originally wanted to broach—the true reason behind his hatred for the Sullivans. The last thing she wanted to hear was still more reasons for her insanity in falling for the man.

She got to her feet and dusted off her butt.

Alarmed, Sully sat up. "Lizzie? Where are you going?"

Now, there was the million dollar question.

She started packing the picnic things. "I don't know, Sully. I honestly don't know."

But this was not working. Every minute she spent with him she fell more in love with the stubborn mule. But it was all on her. He wasn't willing to compromise to be with her. Wasn't willing to give her the only thing she wanted from him other than his love.

And God help her, she couldn't compromise, either.

No, this train was heading down the track to true disaster and she had to get off soon or risk crashing with it. Already, she'd be hurting for a long time. Possibly a lifetime.

"What did I say?" he asked in true bewildered male fashion as he muscled to his feet. "*Mon cœur,* you know I'll give you anything your heart desires. I'm a very wealthy man, thanks to those coins. And Tyree, of course. He recovered our buried treasure and invested…"

The words trailed off as his gaze found hers. "Ah." He pulled the brim of his ball cap over his eyes and stared out over the water.

"Yeah. Ah," she echoed. "It's no use, Sully. We're wasting our—"

"You promised you'd stay," he interrupted, his voice tinged with a shade of boyish petulance, "if I explained my reasons."

"I haven't heard any, yet."

"True," he said, raised his nose and set his frame in an arrogant, spread-footed power stance she was sure in his past had intimidated grown men into obedience and impressionable women to swoon. Even in shorts it was impressive.

But she was beyond intimidation, and she'd never swooned in her life. She hiked her brows.

"I never said *when* I'd explain."

"No," she said stiffly. No wonder the *Sea Nymph* rarely had to fire a shot to capture an enemy vessel. The man was a born negotiator. "And how long do you expect me to wait?"

His gaze slipped from her face and slid down her body, then worked its way up again. Somewhere along the line she'd shed her shirt and shorts, so there was a lot of territory to cover. He paused at her barely covered breasts, which were rosy from the sun and glistened with a sheen of sweat and suntan lotion. Her nipples tightened as though she'd suddenly been transported to the Antarctic.

"Tomorrow," he said.

She blinked. Then her jaw dropped as the inference became clear. "Excuse me?"

"Tomorrow," he repeated.

She stared at him, stunned. "You want me to stay until tomorrow because…?"

"That should be fairly evident."

It was, in fact, evident, and growing more so by the second.

"You would *blackmail* me for a night of sex?" she said incredulously.

What was less obvious, she despaired, was how tempted she was to accept the devil's bargain.

Sully refused to back down, even as he watched Elizabeth's face fill with disbelief. Perhaps horror.

"I *am* a pirate," he reminded her flatly. "And it was you who said all is fair in love and war."

And one thing he'd realized about Elizabeth. She didn't prevaricate or do things halfway. If she was determined to leave, he had no choice. He must discard all his scruples to make sure she didn't.

He wanted her to stay.

He wanted her to be his.

He wanted her any way he could get her.

And what Captain Sullivan Fouquet wanted, one way or another he always got. *Always.* Hadn't he even been brought back from the dead to have his greatest wish fulfilled?

He felt an unwelcome stab of guilt over the fate of Elizabeth's brother. But it was too late—the damage was done. The curse had sealed Caleb Sullivan's destiny long ago. Long before he was born.

"Is that what this is…war?" she asked.

Personally he would have chosen the other alternative. But it was a close call, so whatever worked. He lifted a shoulder. "It doesn't have to be."

She cut him a look. "If I surrender, you mean?"

"If you accept things as they are."

"Not in my nature."

He reached out and caught a strand of her hair being tossed by the breeze, and fingered it. "But surrender is."

A wellspring of vulnerability rose in her eyes for a split second, then she tried to take a step back. In a flash he grasped her behind the neck, preventing her from moving away.

"Sully…" she whispered. "Don't do this."

"Why?" he asked softly, hauling her gently back to him. "You're my woman. I have every right to want you. To enjoy your surrender."

"I'm not your woman," her mouth said, but her eyes said differently.

And to prove it, he pulled her lying mouth against his and kissed her. She gave a weak mewl of protest, tried to pull away, but soon gave in and wrapped her arms around him. As he'd known she would.

"Tomorrow, Elizabeth," he murmured. "Surrender to

me today, and tomorrow we can take up the fight again, if you must."

"I must," she said, but kissed him back.

And then she sweetly surrendered to him. Let him hold her close and kiss her there on the pier in the warm sunshine surrounded by the lapping water and the calling birds and the fragrant smells of summer. And then she let him lead her back to his room and she surrendered all over again, let him hold her close between his cool sheets, surrounded by his yearning body and their hoarse cries and the musky scent of their desire to be one forever.

A desire, he feared, their present course would shatter, as surely as their bodies lay shattered and spent as the sun dipped beneath the horizon, turning today inexorably into tomorrow.

They had a tacit, unspoken agreement not to bring up anything that might divide them. To save it for tomorrow. Tonight, tonight would be their midsummer night's dream, where they could lose themselves in the gossamer spell cast by their lovemaking and pretend the fairy story would never end.

Sully stroked Elizabeth's bare hip as she lay across his chest reading from one of Davey Scraggs's diaries. He was as content as he'd ever been. His body was sated, his hunger quenched and his soul rejoicing from the miracle of this new life he'd been granted and the love he'd found here.

Something warm and wet plopped on his chest. He glanced down in surprise to find her wiping away a tear.

"Hey, what?" he asked.

She smiled and shook her head, embarrassed to be caught. "Nothing. Just being silly."

He took the diary from her and checked the date on the entry she was reading. *Merde.* "You're reading about my death?"

"The funeral, actually. Yours and Tyree's. Your men were quite upset."

Mon Dieu. He touched her cheek with his thumb, wiping away the moisture that clung to her eyelashes. "You mourn a man who just made love to you, *mon coeur.*"

She gave him a watery smile. "Davey wrote some very touching passages."

Moved by her reaction, he pressed a kiss to her lips. He wanted to tell her how much her tears meant to him. How much he loved her sentimentality and softness of heart. How much he loved *her.* But he didn't dare. Tomorrow she would only use it against him.

"You are sweet," he said instead, and kissed her again to disguise his yearning. "Read some more. Aloud for me. But not there." He settled back down on the mattress, pulled her onto his chest and gave her back the journal after turning a few pages forward. "There. I'd like to know what the men did after Tyree and I were gone."

Unfortunately, when she began reading, it couldn't have been from a worse page.

"T'peaceful proceedins was interrupted by an outburst from Gideon Spade t'*Nymph's* boson who claimed he had t'love o' the wench and they was t'be married. Gideon were led away a'shoutin and spent t'nite in gaol for bein in his cups 'n disturbin t'serious-ness o' t'priests pretty readin. Course, t'were all utter rot cuz everone knowt that cap'n Sully was Elizabeth Hayden's betrotht."

Sully froze, comprehension dawning as to what the passage was all about. Fury swept through him. Here was proof positive of her treachery!

But he was snapped back to the present by Elizabeth slamming the book shut and tossing it angrily onto the bed next to her. "Damn it! I just can't get away from that woman, can I?"

He was paralyzed for a moment, caught between wanting to read more, to backtrack to the beginning of this passage in Davey's journal and learn the whole sordid truth of his former fiancée's perfidy, or to soothe the woman lying over him and assure her the other one meant less than nothing.

It was really no contest. He gathered this Elizabeth into his arms and kissed her warmly, tucking away his fury for a more appropriate time. When he was alone.

"Jealous?" he asked lightly, and gave her an unrepentant grin.

She scowled peevishly and smacked his arm. "Not a chance. Whatever gave you that idea?"

"Oh, just a crazy hunch."

She stuck out her bottom lip. "Well, I'm not."

He flipped them on the mattress so she was forced to grab his biceps as she landed under him. "*Bien.* Because, *chère,* you have no reason to be. You're the only woman I want. The only woman I'll ever want again."

Her eyes softened and her arms slid around his neck. "Oh, Sully. If that's true…"

"I know," he murmured. "I'm in big trouble."

"No," she whispered. "We both are."

Chapter 12

When Sully awoke late the next morning, Elizabeth was curled up on the window seat overlooking the back garden, engrossed in another of Davey's diaries. For a moment, he stacked his arms under his head on the pillow and just watched her with a loopy smile.

She was so beautiful. Silhouetted against the blue sky and light green of the foliage, her pale skin appeared porcelain delicate and her blond hair shone like pieces of eight in the morning sun. She'd slipped on one of his white T-shirts, but he could see right through it to the delicious curves of her body. And her legs, her gorgeous long legs, were folded around her luscious bottom, reminding him of how they'd wrapped themselves around his hips for most of the night.

His smile must have changed character during his slow perusal of her body, for when she glanced up and saw it, her lips parted and her cheeks took on a rosy flush.

"Morning," he said.

"You're awake."

"Seems to me I'm still asleep and dreaming of an angel."

The flush deepened, accompanied by a shy smile of pleasure. "Keep talking, pirate man. Flattery will get you everywhere."

"That's what I was hoping." He flipped down the covers. "Come on back over here and I'll whisper some more in your ear."

She dropped the journal and came to him, sliding into his arms as he rolled them and thrust into her in one motion. She greeted his entry with a low moan and held him tight.

This morning he wanted it long and slow. So, true to his word, he began whispering sweet nothings in her ear, along with a few less-than-sweet ones designed to arouse and enflame. It had the desired effect. She was soon breathless.

He made it last and last, bringing her to a peak twice before allowing himself to join her in completion. And when they'd finally come back to earth and lay in each other's arms, she turned to him with dreamy, half-lidded eyes.

"The legend was right," she said.

"About what?" he asked with a content smile.

"You do have voudou."

A million things catapulted through his mind at her

unexpected statement. He lifted up onto his forearms and gazed down at her warily. "Why would you say that?"

"No mere mortal man could make me feel this good. You are amazing."

He let out a nervous laugh. "*Chère,* a man doesn't need voudou to give his woman a good loving."

Her smile turned mischievous. "No wonder Wesley Peel wanted to find the diaries. He was probably hoping for your love potion recipe."

"Now you're being silly."

But she persisted. "A bitter disappointment when he didn't find it, I'm sure. Or maybe he did?" She glanced consideringly over at the stack of diaries on the night-stand. "Hmm."

"Elizabeth, *arrête.* I do not want to talk about voudou."

"Why not?" Suddenly her head cocked as though something occurred to her. Then her eyes widened. "I was right. That's how you did it…. It *is,* isn't it?"

Ah, hell. "Did what, *chère?*"

"Came back to life!"

Merde. He rolled off her onto his back and scrubbed his face. How the devil had she stumbled on to that theory? "I told you, I don't know how it happened. It's not like I asked to be raised from the dead." Not in so many words.

"But when we were at your friend James Tyler's house, you yourself said before he died, Sullivan Fouquet—you—put a voudou curse on Tyree, and—" She sat up with a gasp. "Tyree St. James! He's still alive, too, isn't he? You call your friend James Tyler 'Tyree'…because that's who he really is!"

"Chère," he said evenly. "You are in imminent danger of starting to sound like Wesley Peel."

"Just because he's crazy doesn't mean he's wrong."

She stared at him and he could practically hear the cranks and pulleys of her mind at work. Leading her to a logical conclusion he must not let her reach, at any cost.

"Mon coeur—"

"My God. It all makes sense now."

"No," he said firmly. "It doesn't. Nothing about this situation makes any sense, whatsoever. And blaming it on voudou—"

"So you deny it, then? You're telling me I'm wrong? That the legend is wrong, and that Davey Scraggs and all the men of your crew were also wrong when they whispered about your gift for the curse?"

He scrambled to find an explanation to the unexplainable. One that would satisfy her so she wouldn't pursue the topic any further. "I'm saying they were a bunch of superstitious sailors. And Wesley Peel is a madman. Surely *you* don't believe in such things as curses and the like?"

Her face fell slightly. "Well, I don't believe in transmigration, either," she said pointedly.

He couldn't argue that one. Neither did he, and yet look where he was. He did, however, believe in voudou and his own ability to cast curses. At least...his former ability. He'd seen it work too many times not to believe. His thirst for revenge had been a powerful motivator, and Jeantout had been a powerful teacher. Sully had learned his lessons well.

But now, it seemed, he was paying for them.

Elizabeth was gazing steadily at him, waiting for him to affirm or deny. *God's Bones.*

He calmly got out of bed and began dressing. "I'm hungry. How about you? Why don't we go down and have breakfast."

Her jaw dropped. "So that's it? End of discussion?"

"I don't know what you want me to say."

"Tell me the truth. Did you put a voudou curse on Tyree St. James before you died?"

He jetted out a breath. Debated lying. But couldn't see the point. "Aye. I did."

"And is he still alive?"

"It's more complicated than that. But essentially, aye. He's alive."

"Because of your curse?"

"Elizabeth—"

"Answer the question, Sully."

He folded his arms across his chest. "So he claims." And the details of his ordeal were too closely matched to the words for Sully to have any doubt of it, either. "But only God knows for sure."

"And what about you?"

"Me? Me, I'm hungry. Let's—"

She stepped in front of him, all serious and unwilling to let it go—or him through the door before he'd answered.

"You're messin' with things you should leave well alone, *chère,*" he warned. "You really don't want to get into this."

"But I do. Did you come back to life because of some voudou spell you put on yourself?"

"*Non.* It doesn't work like that," he bit out. Desperately not wanting this to go any further. But not knowing how to stop it. It was like hitting a tidal wave in the middle of the sea—no way around but straight up, and all you could do was pray it didn't break until you were on the other side.

"Then what did it, Sully? Why did you come back?"

He glared at her, and she took an unwilling step backward. She wanted the truth? All right, he'd give it to her. "I'll tell you why I came back," he growled, and leaned down into her face. "Revenge. I came back for revenge."

Elizabeth gasped at the vehemence in Sully's voice as he ground out the word. But before she could recover her wits, he'd swept through the door, making her jump as it slammed hard behind him.

Revenge?

"On whom?"

A sickening nausea crept through her insides as an awful thought occurred to her. He despised the Sullivans…

But no, it couldn't be them. Okay, he may be the illegitimate son of Lord Henry, but that was hardly sufficient reason to hate the family enough to return from the dead for revenge. It didn't add up.

Of course, nothing about this absurd situation added up to anything but insanity.

With a worried mind, she went to her own room and got ready for the day. Then she picked up the phone and called home. Her mom answered. Caleb was still not feeling well, but he wasn't feeling worse, so that was good. After a quick chat with him, she asked to talk to her mother again.

"Can you do something for me?"

"Sure, darling. Anything."

"I can't explain right now, but I really need to know what happened to that servant family, the Fouquets. How and why they left the Sullivan estate."

"A-all right." It was clear her mom was puzzled, but thankfully didn't ask her reason for wanting the information. She honestly didn't know what she would have said. The truth? Scarcely. Her straightforward, logical mom would think she'd gone off the deep end from some mysterious Southern disease.

Yeah. A disease called love.

Elizabeth hung up feeling even more nervous and jumpy than when she'd called. She couldn't shake the instinctive feeling that Sully's need for revenge had something to do with the Sullivans. And she was pretty darn sure she wasn't going to like it when she found out what it was. In fact, she had a sinking feeling it was going to be the final nail in the coffin of their relationship.

Bad analogy. Very bad analogy.

She thought of Caleb, the innocent caught in the middle of all this weirdness, and her heart nearly broke. She could leave Sully today, right now, and she would survive. She'd hurt like hell, but she'd live through it.

She wasn't so sure about Caleb. He needed that bone marrow transplant badly. His slight downturn yesterday was just the beginning. Soon he'd be back in the hospital. And then, how long would he have? Sully was his last chance.

Too bad there wasn't a voudou spell she could cast and—

Oh, my God!

She stood frozen, suddenly dizzy with hope. Sully! He could do it! If he'd brought back Tyree and himself, why not Caleb, too?

Then reality—unreality?—suddenly came crashing back.

He would never do it. If he wouldn't even get a simple blood test, he surely wouldn't cast a voudou spell to save Caleb's life.

Unless… Unless somehow she could make it better. Get him to forgive the Sullivans for whatever harm they'd caused him.

Then, maybe he'd…

She let out a laugh that sounded half hysterical, even to herself. *Voudou?* Was this how desperate she had become? She didn't even believe in it! Admittedly, there was something crazy supernatural going on with Sully. But she was more inclined to believe it was God who'd sent him back to earth to learn an important lesson—one he'd missed last time around—in order to get into heaven.

But…but if there was even a breath of hope for Caleb… She had to try.

So she straightened her spine. And went down to breakfast.

As usual, Mrs. Butterfield chattered on as she served them a scrumptious morning feast of ham and grits, waffles with maple syrup and plenty of rich, aromatic coffee. Sully had to admit, he'd never eaten so well in his life as he had for the past several days here at the Pirate's Rest Inn.

Nor had the company been as agreeable. Mrs. Butterfield was always agreeable, of course. And Elizabeth was trying very hard to be pleasant. Even though she hadn't yet looked him in the eye.

"So," asked Mrs. B. "What are you two up to this morning?"

"Physical therapy," he answered cheerfully. "Every morning at ten for the foreseeable future, I'm afraid." He glanced at the wall clock. "Jake called and said he'd pick me up at nine-thirty."

"And what about you, dear?" she asked Elizabeth.

There was a slight pause. "Oh, I thought I'd visit the cemetery. I want to see Sullivan Fouquet's grave."

He dropped his coffee cup.

"Oh, my goodness!" Mrs. Butterfield exclaimed, running for a cloth and dabbing the hot liquid that had splashed his shirt.

"I'm so sorry, Mrs. B.," he said, cutting Elizabeth a scowl. What was the woman up to now? "How clumsy of me."

"Not to worry, it'll wash out. Did you burn yourself?"

"I'm fine."

"Well, Elizabeth," Mrs. Butterfield said, disposing of the stained linen. "I think that's a splendid idea. The graves are quite spectacular."

"Graves?" his lover asked, too innocently for his liking. "Fouquet has more than one?"

Sully grimaced. Tyree had warned him that some

town committee thirty years ago had moved his and Elizabeth Hayden's graves together. Better for the tourist trade, they'd decided. More in line with the romantic myth of tragic lovers that Maybelle Chadbourne's penny dreadful novel had created. The stone monument they'd erected was…different…according to Clara. Tyree had just laughed and mumbled something about the advantages of being the villain of the story.

"Oh, yes," Mrs. Butterfield continued earnestly. "Poor Captain Fouquet and his beloved fiancée, Elizabeth— Oh! What a coincidence! That's your name, too!"

"Yes, imagine that," Elizabeth said with a smile. "Do go on."

"Poor Captain Fouquet and his beloved Elizabeth were cut down in their prime by his dastardly partner, Captain St. James." She shuddered dramatically. "Such a dreadful man."

Sully snorted eloquently.

Mrs. Butterfield looked offended. "He *was* dreadful! The philandering rogue shot Miss Elizabeth in cold blood!"

"Perhaps she deserved it," Sully couldn't resist saying, though naturally he didn't really believe that. It just irritated him having his colossal stupidity carved in stone for all to witness.

Mrs. Butterfield gasped in outrage. "Well!"

"Ignore him, Mrs. B. He's been in a snarky mood all morning. You were saying about the fiancée?"

"Ah, she was the town beauty. And—"

"I am not in a snarky mood," he muttered.

"—the captain loved her very much. After St. James shot her, she died in—"

"Just because I don't want to talk about voudou," he grumbled under his breath.

"—his arms. It was so romant—" Their hostess blinked. "Voudou?"

Nothing got past the old bat.

He plastered a smile onto his lips. "Aye, apparently Miz Hamilton, here, believes in spells and curses. Now, me, I—"

"You—" Elizabeth jumped up in outrage, poking her finger at him "—are such a… Such a hyp—" Suddenly she snapped her mouth shut, plopped back down on her chair, smiled brightly and turned back to Mrs. Butterfield. "You were saying about Sullivan Fouquet and his dear sweetheart?"

Mrs. B looked from Elizabeth's perky smile to his stormy frown and back again. And probably decided she'd have no part of whatever lunacy was going on between them. No doubt she knew they were sleeping together—that wasn't the kind of thing one could hide from an innkeeper—and chalked it up to a lovers' tiff.

Their hostess drew herself up and said very primly. "It's true. They were very much in love. Devoted to one another. It was a terrible thing, their true love being cut short like that."

Elizabeth nodded solemnly. "They sound like the perfect couple. Well. Except for the bloodthirsty pirate part."

"Privateer," Sully said between his teeth. "And she was—"

Elizabeth ignored him and blithely continued, "Would you mind if I cut some roses from your garden, Mrs. Butterfield? I'd like to place them on my namesake's grave."

Sully slapped his hands on the table so hard the china cups threatened to jump out of the saucers. "You will *not*—"

If he could have turned Elizabeth—this one—over his knee right then he would have done so with relish. But since that was out of the question—for the moment—he marshaled his ire and gave her an imperious look. "I think I hear Jake's truck pulling up in front and I forgot the backpack with the journals upstairs. Would you mind getting it for me?"

Reluctantly she lifted her chin and went up to fetch it. When she returned and held it out to him, he took her arm instead, and said, "I'd like you to come with me."

She balked, but he didn't give her an option. He simply propelled her out the door and down the front steps.

"Sully! Let me go this instant," she ground out as he pulled her down the path. "I don't want to go with you."

"And I don't want you to go to my grave. *Flowers for your namesake? Mon Dieu,* what has gotten into you? If you are still angry about this morning, I'm sorry I was rude. I don't like talking about voudou."

"That's all well and good, but *I* don't—"

Luckily they'd arrived at the curb where Jake was waiting in his truck and she couldn't complete the thought. Sully wrenched open the door and deposited her on the bench seat, then climbed in beside her, forcing her to the middle. "Hope you don't mind if Elizabeth comes along?" he said after greeting Jake.

"Not a problem." The other man hiked a brow at her churlish expression and tightly crossed arms, but didn't comment. "After I drop you off I'm headed for Morrisey Island. I'm meeting Professor Rouse there to go over some details about the fire."

Elizabeth's face immediately animated. "Oh! Can I come with you? There's something— I mean, I've never been to a fire scene and would love to see what you do. I promise not to get in the way."

The woman truly must think him an idiot. "I'm sure Jake will be far too busy to—"

"Hell, she can come along if she wants. It's probably pretty boring hanging around the hospital waiting for you."

To his astonishment, she turned and twined her arms around Sully's neck, then gave him a long kiss that could leave little doubt as to what they'd spent the night doing. "Please, darling? I won't bother Jake at all, I swear."

After that head-spinning kiss, he could hardly say no without appearing an unreasonable boor. Which was doubtless exactly what she was counting on.

He grasped her jaw in his hand just hard enough to get her attention. "No bothering Professor Rouse, either," he said intently. It was fairly obvious what she had in mind. "The man just lost his home. He won't want to engage in a discussion of voudou with you."

"Voudou?" Jake asked in surprise. "You interested in voudou?"

"Because of the arsonist," she explained, lifting the backpack she still held. "I heard that Wesley Peel may have been collecting these old diaries to find the words to a voudou curse Sullivan Fouquet put on Tyree St. James. I thought that was interesting."

Jake nodded. "Yes, I've considered that theory. But Peel was also stealing paintings by an artist named Thom Bowden. The two things don't seem to mesh."

Sully thought otherwise. Back when Thom Bowden had been a regular patron of the Moon and Palmetto and sketched Sully and Tyree for coin, their crews also frequently sat as his subjects—including Davey Scraggs. Thom Bowden had done the pencil drawing of their treasure island with which Elizabeth Hayden had planned to betray them. And according to the diary, Wesley Peel's ancestor John Peel was the very one who'd followed Sully and Tyree to the island.

It was all too incestuous to be a coincidence.

"It's about money," Sully said. "Not voudou. Tyree's—James Tyler's research proved that John Peel recovered one of Fouquet's treasure chests and used the gold to establish his lumber mill. He must have left some private family papers telling about finding the treasure, and now that Wesley Peel has lost the mill, he's hoping to find more of it."

Elizabeth gave him a penetrating look. "But he won't, will he?"

"Non," he said levelly. "There is no more treasure to be found." So she had been listening yesterday.

Jake chuckled. "How do you know that? Did you find it?"

The devil. He grinned, and winked at Jake. "*Non,* James Tyler did. How do you think he could afford that incredible estate he lives on and to go gallivanting off on a year-long honeymoon?"

Jake laughed at that, as he was supposed to. "Yeah, right."

"Okay, then how do you explain the painting?" Elizabeth said, interrupting their banter. "The one Wesley Peel was stealing from the Moon and Palmetto when he set the fire that injured you?"

"Yeah," Jake said, sobering. "That bothers me, too. Peel stole that painting *after* he had all the journals. And now, this fire at Professor Rouse's place. Why set that at all?"

"Admittedly," Sully conceded, "these last incidents don't fit."

"Which is why," Jake said, pulling up in front of the Old Fort Mystic Medical Center to drop him off, "I'm going to talk to the professor."

Reluctantly, Sully got down from the truck and turned back to Elizabeth. "I'd like you to stay here with me."

"Don't worry," she said, the stubborn light in her eyes telling him if he tried to argue he'd lose. "Jake will take good care of me." She leaned down and gave him a kiss goodbye.

"Why don't you keep the backpack with you?" Jake suggested. "A little light reading in case we're late picking you up. See if you can find any more clues."

With an irritated exhale, he waved and helplessly watched them drive off. He had a bad feeling about that.

She wanted to talk to the voudou expert, and he could only shudder to think what she might learn.

And what she might ask Sully when she returned.

Chapter 13

Elizabeth waited patiently while Jake asked Professor Rouse a million questions about the fire, about what he'd seen and about what Peel—whom he always referred to as "the suspect"—might have been after.

"I can't imagine what he could have wanted from me. I'm a college professor, not a rich man."

"No expensive collections? No valuable or rare books?"

"The only things I collected were related to my research."

"On voudou?" Elizabeth chimed in, trying not to let her eagerness to ask her own questions show.

"Yes, exactly," Professor Rouse said. "I have…had," he corrected sadly, "an extensive collection of voudou artifacts and a ton of books, but they are…were not terribly valuable. The most expensive was probably worth a couple hundred dollars. Besides, why would anyone burn down a house if their aim was to steal valuables from it?"

Jake pursed his lips. "Our suspect is unbalanced. We think when he doesn't find exactly what he's looking for, he torches the place in a rage."

"Jeezus," Rouse said, rubbing a hand over his face. "But what specifically was he after?"

Elizabeth listened as Jake asked about any old journals or paintings the professor might own, all with the same answer. Nothing.

"I think he was looking for you," she said when the two men's exchange reached a dead end.

They both turned to her in surprise.

"Me?"

"How do you figure?" Jake asked.

"Sully's friend James Tyler thinks the arsonist is trying to cast a voudou spell or curse. I'm not sure why. It may be about getting money, or possibly something else. But the arsonist found an old diary containing the words to a voudou curse that reputedly worked."

"So you think he wanted to force me to show him how to use it?" Rouse asked, his expression half intrigued, half horrified.

"You're an expert. Could you? Show him?" she asked, and held her breath for his answer.

His mouth opened and closed a couple of times. "Well," he finally said, "that depends."

Her breath whooshed out. "On what?"

"On whether the man in question has voudou."

"Huh?" Jake said, confused.

"By having voudou," Rouse explained, "I mean possessing the power to make voudou work. No one really knows how you get it. Many believe you have to be born with it. Lots of people try casting spells and curses. Nearly all fail."

"Do you have it?" Elizabeth asked, carefully hiding her excitement.

"Me?" The professor shook his head wryly. "No, I just study the phenomenon. To have voudou I think you really have to believe. I'm too much of a scientist to truly believe."

Disappointment stabbed through her. "But you've seen it work?"

"Absolutely."

"So how do you explain that?" she asked in frustration.

"I can't," he said. "That's what makes it all so fascinating."

"You don't think it's merely the power of suggestion?" Jake asked, for which Elizabeth was grateful. She felt close to a meltdown.

"Certainly, in some instances, maybe even in most, that's exactly what it is. But there have been cases..." The professor shook his head, clearly captivated by his subject. "Some instances just have no rational explanation. At least that we've discovered."

"Yet," Jake said firmly.

Rouse smiled so his eyes twinkled. "Yeah. Yet."

"So," Elizabeth persisted, the need to have an answer burning in the pit of her stomach, "in those instances where it's not suggestion, are you saying it's not the spell or the curse, the words themselves, that have the power, but the person who says them?"

"That seems to be the case. Often it's hereditary, practitioners passing on their gift to a son or daughter, but not always. Some just have it."

All her hope deflated. "And no one knows how those people get their power?"

"Correct. Although…" He hesitated.

Her heart began to pound. "Yes?"

"There seems to be a correlation between very strong abilities and an unusually potent emotional motivator."

Oh God. Blood rushed through her veins. "Such as?"

"Such as love—nearly always unrequited—or fury over a terrible injustice. But the most common factor is…" He clamped his teeth, gazing out over the still smoking remains of his home.

She didn't want to hear it. Not really. Because somehow she knew exactly what he was about to say. But this was why she'd come—to get to the bottom of the truth about Sully. "Yes, Professor? The most common factor is?"

The professor turned and gave her a wan smile. "Revenge, young lady. Those with the greatest power for voudou feel the greatest need for personal revenge."

They were late. Naturally.

Sully settled down in a cushy hospital reception area chair to wait for Jake and Elizabeth and opened the backpack. What the hell. He'd wanted to leaf through the journals anyway.

He pulled out a stack and shuffled through them,

reading the years written on the front covers. Which to choose? Did he feel like reminiscing over old times, or did he want to know what had happened to his ship and crew after his death? Or maybe he should look for clues to the fires.

In the end, because his reading skills were so laborious, he decided to just skim down the pages with his forefinger, stopping to read only when he ran across something that piqued his interest, such as the names Elizabeth, John Peel, Thom Bowden and that rat bastard, Gideon Spade.

Even after all his fiancée's treachery, Sully still felt a spike of fury at the man for stealing what was his. And making plans to steal *everything* that was his. For surely, Gideon was behind the plan to steal the treasure as well as Elizabeth.

He found a few more references to Gideon's lamentations over her untimely demise, much to Davey's disdain. Good man. Certainly there was enough to convince Sully he'd been right about his fiancée's faithlessness. How could he ever have thought himself in love with the scheming wench? How could he ever have compared the present Elizabeth to her? The thought made him ill. For all the complications and impossibilities of their relationship, Elizabeth Hamilton's emotions and feelings for him were real and true and never hidden.

He banked his despondency over his bad luck with both Elizabeths and continued to skim the journal. Five pages later he ran across a passage that made him sit straight up in his seat:

T'nite the Moon and Palmetto were all in an
uproar on account o' young Billy McManus swore
he seed one o' the old dead Capns, Capn Tyree,
walkin about the village a'ter dark like he were
still alive. Young Billy took a bad fright 'n were
shakin all nite. The men ar wisperin about Capn
Sully's curse. T'is the voudou, I tell ye. I warned
him his dealins with that Haitian devil Jeantout
would come to no good. An' now pur Capn Tyree
is a curst soul, God bless him.

Sully let out a long, uneven breath. So this was the
origin of the legend. Tyree had told him how he'd
stumbled about in a daze for weeks after their deaths,
wondering why no one could see or hear him. Apparently only a very few mortals had been able to perceive
Tyree's physical being while he was still in his cursed,
undead state. Young Billy must have been one of the
unlucky few. How many others had there been over the
years? Tyree's wife, Clara, had been one and Mrs. Yates.
And apparently also Wesley Peel.

Sully got to thinking. Had that been what set Peel off
on his rampage to find the infamous voudou curse—that
somehow he'd spotted Tyree's restless spirit walking
around Magnolia Cove, and put that living proof
together with the legend of Sully's voudou?

Sully leafed through the journals and found a few
more references to Tyree sightings. A serving girl at a
remote estate who insisted he was haunting the attic,
a cabin boy on the *Sea Sprite* who fell overboard and
swore it was Tyree who'd rescued him. A solicitor who

lived in Tyree's old apartments and woke one night to see him banging on the wall behind the bed—probably trying to get into the hidey-hole. All carefully recorded by Davey Scraggs.

No doubt he'd just as carefully recorded some of the mysterious incidents that happened while Sully was still alive—all after the rescue of Jeantout from the Haitian rebellion. Incidents where enemies who had caused horrific cruelties to women or children suddenly experienced terrible deaths. Owners of the slave vessels he'd freed who'd died screaming their remorse. All it had taken was a simple incantation whispered by Sully and their fates were decided. He hadn't had to lift a finger, and his curses had all come to pass.

Little wonder the legend of his preternatural powers had taken root and grown. He wondered if he still held those powers. If they'd transferred to Andre Sullivan's body along with Sully's memories and soul.

Oddly enough, he hoped they hadn't. It was a grave responsibility having the power of life and death over a person. *Dieu,* even life *after* death. In the past he never abused his power. At least he hadn't felt he had. He'd used it only on people who were so cruel, so bereft of human morals and ethics that society would have condemned them, too, had the full extent of their terrible deeds been known to all.

But… Because of Tyree and Elizabeth Hamilton… and Caleb…he was learning that his actions had ramifications he'd never considered. With Tyree it had been just blind jealousy that had produced the ill-conceived curse, and Tyree had suffered for it for two hundred years. With

Lord Henry, Sully had wanted to cause him pain and sorrow, in retribution for his parents' pain and his sister's sorrow. But he now realized that curse was also causing innocent people, women and children whom he had only wanted to protect, equal pain and sorrow.

He no longer wished to have that power.

He sighed and stared up at the ceiling.

Had his need for revenge softened? *Non.* It still burned like a volcano in his gut. But only for one man. Lord Henry. It wasn't Sully's place to judge anyone else. He understood that now.

And vowed he would never, ever utter a single word of a voudou curse again, no matter how tempted he might be.

When Jake and Elizabeth came to pick him up, Sully greeted her with a kiss and Jake by tossing him the backpack. The physio was going well and he was able to walk as far as the truck carrying his stick instead of leaning on it. All around, he was feeling pretty damn good.

"How did it go with the professor?" he asked when they were on the road to Magnolia Cove.

Jake pursed his lips and Elizabeth folded her arms across her chest. "I still say Peel was looking for a voudou curse, not treasure," she stated emphatically.

Jake glanced at Sully wryly. "We've been debating the case. Seems we disagree on motive."

"Because of the professor?" Sully asked curiously.

"In spite of the professor," Elizabeth answered. "Even though Rouse is an expert on voudou, Jake still thinks finding treasure is Peel's motive."

"True, Rouse didn't own any of Scraggs's diaries or

Thom Bowden's paintings," Jake interjected. "But Peel *did* burn down the house. He only does that when he's frustrated by *not* finding what he's looking for."

Elizabeth's expression went stubborn. "That could equally apply to Professor Rouse himself. Peel didn't find *him,* either, since he didn't arrive home until after the fire was burning."

They both turned to Sully, and at the same time Jake said, "What do you think, Andre?" Elizabeth said, "What do you think, Sully?"

God's Teeth. "Perhaps you should call me Sully from now on, too," he said to Jake. "As for Peel's motive...I don't know that we can say either way for sure at this point."

"Thanks loads, *Sully,*" Jake muttered.

"I can't believe you're saying that," Elizabeth persisted. She grabbed a beat-up accordion file from the dashboard and riffled through the pages. "In reading through the case file on the way back, I found this e-mail that Peel had sent to antique book dealers and auction sites around the country. He was searching specifically for the journal written the year Sullivan Fouquet and Tyree St. James had their duel and died."

"The volume Clara found at the Pirate Museum and he later stole from her," Jake said. "So?"

"So, that journal was in the backpack and I read it cover to cover yesterday. There isn't one mention of any secret hiding place for any treasure. Not Sullivan Fouquet's or anyone else's."

They all digested that as Jake made a left turn onto the Frenchman's Island road.

"Tyler left me his notes about the case," Sully offered. "I remembered a reference to a passage where Davey says Wesley Peel's ancestor, John Peel, bragged about following Fouquet and St. James out to their buried cache. In a journal written five years after they died."

"That's strange," Elizabeth said, setting the file back on the dashboard. "Why would John Peel wait five whole years to claim the treasure if he was the one who'd followed them to its hiding place while they were alive?"

Sully shook his head. "No idea."

"Could he have gotten sick, or gone on a long sea voyage?"

"*Non.* John was mentioned several times in the years in between. Healthy and living at home."

"I still think it's about the treasure," Jake said. "Greed, love and revenge. Those are the most common motives for a crime. I'm not seeing the last two, so my money is on the first."

Sully winced inwardly at his mention of revenge, but didn't have time to ponder it because Jake swerved to miss a dog that ran into the street, and the accordion file landed in Sully's lap spilling its contents onto his thighs.

As he tucked the pages back into the folder, one of them caught his eye. It was a slick color flyer, an advertisement for the Moon and Palmetto pub. In the center of the page staring out from a fancy portrait were himself and Tyree looking as bloodthirsty as they ever did in real life. Behind them were the *Sea Nymph* and *Sea Sprite* in full sail, passing in front of a palmetto-bedecked island—which Sully instantly recognized.

The treasure island.

"I'll be damned. What is this painting?" he asked.

Jake glanced over. "That's the one they were unveiling at the Moon and Palmetto during the Pirate Festival the night of the fire. The one Wesley Peel stole. Why?"

"Just curious," he murmured. It wasn't like he could tell Jake about the island. There would be no way to explain how he knew what it was and no way to prove it.

"Quite a resemblance, eh?"

"What?"

"Between you and Fouquet." Jake grinned. "You always did get a lot of mileage out of that. Remember?"

"Um, thankfully no." Sully winked at Elizabeth as he tucked the flyer back into the folder. "Unless…didn't you once mention a thing for pirates, *chère?*"

She blushed prettily. "Certainly not."

Jake rolled his eyes. "See what I mean? I better drop you two off before it gets embarrassing."

"Just pull in at the fire house," he told him with a chuckle. "We can walk back to the Inn. You don't mind, do you?" he asked her.

"Of course not. There's a stop or two I'd like to make anyway."

Jake parked and Sully passed the file over to him. "Good luck figuring it all out. Let me know if I can help."

After saying goodbye, he and Elizabeth turned and started walking toward home.

Home.

Now there was a concept Sully had never properly thought about before. Probably because he'd never really had a home. Not since his family was torn apart so long ago.

He put his arm around Elizabeth's shoulder and kissed her hair. "I missed you," he said, and realized it was more true than he'd like to admit. Every minute they were apart he missed talking to her, missed the sight of her smile, the scent of her, the small touches they exchanged and the sensual ones. Missed the sweet taste of her lips on his.

"I missed you, too," she said smiling up at him, and he prayed she truly meant it.

He gathered her to him and pulled her close for a long, yearning kiss. "Ah, Elizabeth, what are we—"

Just then, the Magnolia Cove fire truck rumbled by on the way to pulling into the station. Four firefighters leaned out the windows wolf-whistling and waving with big grins on their faces.

"Hey, Chief! You go for it, man!"

Sully winced. Jake may have noticed he'd changed since the fire, but obviously the other men hadn't. Not that it bothered him so much anymore. They'd catch on soon enough.

"Where y'all been?" he shouted back, keeping his arms firmly around Elizabeth. The dispatcher hadn't informed him of any fire today.

"Rose Cottage," Jeremy Swift yelled. "False alarm."

Rose Cottage? That was Tyree's place! Where Mrs. Yates was living all alone while he and Clara were on their honeymoon. The hair on the back of Sully's neck started to prickle. "Mrs. Yates all right?" he called.

"She's fine. Just that new-fangled alarm system Tyler installed before sailing off into the sunset," Jeremy grumbled good-naturedly. "What the heck, it's a nice day for a ride on a fire truck."

Sully glanced at Elizabeth. She looked worried, too. "Feel like taking a drive out there?"

She nodded. "The Corvette's parked at the Pirate's Rest."

One of these days he really would have to learn how to drive it himself. Meanwhile, he was glad she could. The alarm was probably just being oversensitive, as the guys had said, but he had a queasy feeling in his stomach about this. He'd had that queasy feeling many a time in the past.

And he never ignored it.

All looked peaceful as they drove up to Rose Cottage about fifteen minutes later. No sign of smoke, thank God.

Elizabeth drove slowly, taking in the enormous beauty of the estate. She still couldn't get over how gorgeous the Southern sea islands were. Spanish moss hung from huge, stately oaks, swaying gently in the soft breeze, along with the fronds of the palmettos that clustered between. The scent of jasmine filled the air, spiced with a tang of sea salt and the sticky marsh ooze the locals called pluff mud—the unique smell of the Lowcountry that she'd grown to love after only a few days. So much richer and more verdant than the stark pine and cold ocean smells of her northern home.

As the tires crunched up the oyster shell path to the beautiful plantation home, a pair of bluebirds flew out from the trees bordering a meadow on one side of the track, making their distinctive call.

Beside her, Sully scanned the whole area, looking for signs of anything amiss. "Nothing out of place," he said, but she could tell he was still tense.

When Mrs. Yates appeared on the front porch, smiled and waved, they both relaxed a little.

"We heard about your excitement," Sully said when they'd gotten out of the car and walked up the steps. He gave her a kiss on the cheek. "Came to make sure you're really okay."

"Oh, heavens," she said, laughing. "You didn't have to do that. Just another of Captain Tyr—that is, Captain Tyler's fancy gadgets. You just have to look at it wrong to set the darn thing off. Most annoying."

"I'm happy to hear it wasn't a real emergency," he said, offering his arm to escort her inside and beckoning Elizabeth to follow. Then to her shock, he said, "Mrs. Yates, Elizabeth knows about me and Tyree, so you don't have to guard your words around her anymore."

The older woman's brows shot up in surprise. "Indeed, Captain? Well. That's very interesting. You must join me for some tea and tell me how that happened." She looked from him to Elizabeth, who followed behind feeling vaguely unnerved. "I can't imagine you've had an easy time accepting any of this, my dear."

"No," she agreed. "And I'm still not sure I have."

Mrs. Yates chuckled and Sully looked wounded. "That's not what you said last night."

She felt her face go red, but Mrs. Yates rescued her. "I imagine some things are far more believable in the quiet arms of the night than faced in the bright light of daytime."

Sully smiled as she patted his hand and headed for the tea kettle. "That was very poetical, Mrs. Yates. And undoubtedly true."

A cool breeze rustled the lace curtains on the kitchen windows, making delicate shadows waltz across the pastel yellow walls and glass-front cabinets. It was a lovely kitchen. Suddenly it struck Elizabeth that she'd like to have just such a cozy kitchen someday, when she married. She glanced at Sully, and was pierced by a poignant sadness. Too bad if she ever did marry, it wouldn't be to this amazing man.

"Did the captain tell you who he was?" Mrs. Yates asked, handing her the cups to set out, "Or did you guess?"

Elizabeth snapped out of her wishful thinking. "A little of both, I guess. I knew about Sully's amnesia and him waking up from his coma thinking he was…well, who he is. And he seemed to know everything about Sullivan Fouquet. Then there's his Cajun accent. Oh, and finding the gold coins. That was pretty convincing."

"Coins?" Mrs. Yates asked.

"Hidden in my old town house," Sully said. "I had a secret cache even Tyree didn't know about."

"Goodness!" Mrs. Yates chuckled. "They must be worth a pretty penny by now."

"We got there just in time," Elizabeth said. "Later that day the building burned down."

Suddenly there was a crash, like a glass jar falling from a shelf and shattering.

Sully whipped around and listened intently.

"The pantry!" Mrs. Yates whispered.

"Did the firefighters check the whole house before they left?"

"Yes, indeed. At least, I thought…"

A soft crunch came from the same direction, as though someone had stepped on the broken glass.

"Call Jake," Sully whispered over his shoulder, but Elizabeth was already reaching for her cell phone. "Does Tyree keep any weapons in the house?"

"I—I don't think so," Mrs. Yates said, her voice wobbling slightly. "He doesn't approve of them."

Another crunch sounded.

"Do you even know how to use a modern gun?" Elizabeth whispered worriedly.

Sully gave her a quelling scowl. "Take Mrs. Yates and go out the back door. Get to the boathouse and stay there. Now!"

She hesitated, but he made a shooing motion and Mrs. Yates looked like she was about to expire on the spot. "Please be careful," she whispered to Sully, holding his eyes for a moment, then she put her arm around the older woman's shoulders and quietly led her out the back door.

As they hurried down the old brick path toward the dock and the boathouse, she dialed 911 and asked the operator to put her through to the Magnolia Cove Fire Department.

Jake wasn't there. But a man named Swift answered and said they'd be at Rose Cottage in five minutes.

Elizabeth and Mrs. Yates reached the boathouse, and after checking to be sure they were alone, she urged Mrs. Yates inside. It was cool and dark and smelled of motor oil and fish. As Elizabeth was swinging the door closed behind them, she noticed a small motorboat bobbing on the water, tied up at the dock next to the boathouse.

"Is that yours?" she asked Mrs. Yates.

"Why, no, I don't think so." She peeped out at it between the weathered wood doors. "No, I've never seen that boat before."

Proof that someone was here who didn't belong. *Wesley Peel?* But what would he want at Rose Cottage? The painting in the hall? *Sully?*

She hesitated for only a second. "Stay here," she told Mrs. Yates, then ran out onto the dock. When she got to the boat, she jumped down onto the back, next to where the motor had been tipped up out of the water. Squinting at the workings, she poked around and found what looked like a fuel line.

Just as she yanked it from the motor, the quiet morning was ripped apart by a loud bang.

Her heart stopped, then jumped to her throat as she realized the sound had come from the house.

She spun around. Another bang split the air.

Someone was shooting!

Chapter 14

Sully dove to the floor and rolled through the nearest door, scrambling to find a piece of furniture to hide behind.

"I know who you are!" Wesley Peel shouted as he burst from the pantry and gave chase. "I know *what* you are!"

That made one of them. Sully scanned the cozy front salon where he'd landed. A fireplace, a sofa and a three soft, stuffed chairs that looked like they wouldn't stop a determined dog, much less a bullet. *Merde.* He scooted behind one of the chairs. The sofa was too exposed, facing the fireplace. His knee started to burn and he grimaced.

"Give me what I want, Fouquet!" Peel screeched as he rounded the door. He cackled wildly. "I'll be your loyal servant…"

Dieu. The man was insane.

From his hiding place, Sully examined the room, looking for potential weapons. *Two end tables. Several potted plants. Brass fireplace implements.* That was good. One looked sharp with a hook, like a small harpoon. *A few vases scattered on the mantel.* Then his eye snagged on what was mounted above it. *The crossed sabers.* His and Tyree's old weapons; he'd noticed them there on his first visit. Slowly a smile creased his face.

"Surrender, Fouquet! Or I'll kill the old lady and your pretty friend! I know where they're hiding!"

Touch them and you're dead, mon ami. Gritting his teeth against the pain in his awkwardly held leg, Sully reached up on to the windowsill behind the chair and hefted one of the clay-potted plants into his hand. He threw it to the opposite side of the room, where it crashed into bits.

Peel swung and fired madly, pumping bullets into an empty chair. As stuffing flew everywhere, Sully grabbed the brass harpoon from the hearth and rolled in front of the sofa.

Peel slowly turned in a circle, growling, "Give me what I need, Fouquet, and I'll let the women live."

Sully debated whether he should let *him* live. Lying on the floor, he could look under the sofa and see Peel's feet as he searched the room for him. That would have to do for now. Grasping the heavy brass poker, Sully aimed at Peel's ankle and sent it sailing.

Direct hit.

Peel yowled and bent to grab his bloody limb. Meanwhile Sully jumped up and yanked the sabers from their wall mounting. Tyree's slid into his left hand and his own sword hilt glided into his right palm, reassuring and familiar in its weight and girth.

"Devil!" Peel screamed. "Voudou demon! I want you to *curse* me, not kill me!"

"Then what good would killing me do? You're a madman, Peel! "

Apparently beyond reason, the other man staggered to his feet and raised the gun. "Shut up!" Instinctively Sully lifted Tyree's sword in a protective stance just as the trigger jerked. Sparks flew in a blinding flash and the flat of the saber slapped viciously against Sully's chest.

Someone screamed. A woman. *Elizabeth!*

Knocked momentarily breathless by the blow, Sully could only watch, helpless, as Peel swung to see her in the hall behind him. Instantly Peel grabbed her around the neck, pointing the barrel of the gun at her temple as he turned back, using her as a shield.

Sully let the tips of the sabers drop to the floor. "Hurt her and I'll curse you to the eternal fires of hell," he gritted out, seething with fury over the terror in Elizabeth's eyes. He wanted to smash the man's face in. He wanted to slice him to ribbons. He gripped his sword hilt, ready to do just that if Peel made one move to hurt her.

"What do you want from me, Peel?"

"Same as you have," the man said, his voice high with fanatical excitement. "Eternal life!"

Sully barked a laugh. "Is that what you think?"

"You're Sullivan Fouquet, aren't you? You said so in all the newspapers. And Sullivan Fouquet died two hundred years ago! But you came back to life."

"I'm Andre Sullivan, the fire chief. You know that, Peel.

I was injured back then. On pain meds and delirious. Now let Elizabeth go before you do something you'll regret."

"I just shot you!" he yelled. "And you didn't die! It's voudou, I tell you! You're immortal!"

Sully glanced down at the thin, saber-curved line of blood bisecting his chest where it had kicked back at him. "The sword deflected the bullet. No voudou involved." But possibly a miracle. He prayed for one more.

"Don't lie to me! I need to know the secret! I've said the words over and over, but nothing happens!" He pushed his gun harder into Elizabeth's temple. "Tell me!"

Inwardly boiling with rage, Sully forced himself not to move an inch. "I can't tell you what I don't know. Besides, I thought this was about money. About saving your family business."

For a second, the man's eyes lost their dangerous, glossy wildness. "It was. In the beginning. But now I—"

"The painting," Sully interrupted Peel's rising voice. "The one from the Moon and Palmetto. You took that to lead you to the treasure. The island in the background, that's where it's buried! What you've been looking for all along. Why stop now?"

Elizabeth squirmed, and Peel tightened his grip on her neck. "Hold still!" The crazed look returned to his eyes. "No! It's too late. Finding that painting was taking too long! Then I learned about your voudou from the journals. And I thought, what good are riches if you die before spending them?"

"Peel—"

"Curse me to eternal life and I'll let her go!" he said shrilly. The man was completely around the bend.

Enough of this. Time to act. Sully tightened his fingers around the hilts of the sabers. Elizabeth caught the slight movement and met his eyes. He gave an imperceptible nod.

"I need a lock of your hair," he told Peel levelly. "For the spell to work."

Peel frowned. "You're lying. There was nothing about hair in the curse you put on Tyree St. James."

"That curse was not for eternal life."

"I don't believe you!"

Sully shrugged. "*Bon.* Then let the woman go. We're done here." He started boldly walking toward the front door. Getting closer.

Peel dropped his jaw and his guard, and the gun dipped just long enough for Sully to make his move. He whipped around and lunged, Tyree's saber slicing through the air to knock the gun from Peel's hand and send it clattering into the hall. At the same time Elizabeth lifted her foot and slammed her heel into his injured ankle. He howled and lost his grip on her. She collapsed to the floor, giving Sully's saber full access to Peel's neck.

In a twinkling, he had backed the man up against the wall, the tip of his sword pushing into the base of Peel's throat. He barely restrained himself from running the man through.

"Move and you are dead," he ground out. "Lizzie, are you all right?"

"I'm good," she answered shakily from where she sat on the floor, arms banded around her middle. "Your men should be here any—"

The front door burst open and Jake ran in. "Andre!" He took one look at the scene and came to a screeching halt. "Everyone okay here?"

Peel's Adam's apple bobbed under Sully's saber tip, his wide eyes appealing desperately to Jake. "Don't you see it's Sullivan Fouquet!" he squeaked hysterically. "He's a devil! Cursed! He promised me eternal life!"

Jake's eyebrows flicked. "Sure he did." He pulled a pair of handcuffs from his belt. "But first we'd better make sure you're safe from him, being a devil and all."

Sully eased up and let him cuff the bastard. As soon as Peel was secured, Sully set the swords aside and dropped down at Elizabeth's side, tugging her trembling body into a fierce embrace. "Where's Mrs. Yates?"

"B-boathouse," she stuttered.

Jake nodded. "I'll get her." Then he pushed Peel down the hall and out the front door.

Sully turned to Elizabeth, buried his face in her hair. "I wanted to kill him," he confessed intently, holding her close, hating how her heartbeat raced and her hands shook as she clung to him. "I wanted to draw and quarter the bastard and throw the pieces to the sharks for what he did to you."

Her body gave a long shudder, then calmed. "I may have let you," she murmured. "Except I felt so sorry for the man. He obviously needs help." She pulled back. "Thank you for rescuing me." She smiled gamely. "My hero."

He pulled her back for another hug. "I don't know what I would have done if he'd hurt you."

She pulled in a breath, then let it out. "He wouldn't have. You were pretty handy with those swords."

"One of the few advantages of being two centuries behind the times." She smiled and he gave her a kiss, needing the reassurance that she really was all right, knowing her touch would tell him the truth. "You were very brave, *mon amour.*"

The front door opened again and Mrs. Yates walked in accompanied by Jeremy Swift and another Magnolia Cove firefighter.

"Oh, dear! Such excitement!" Mrs. Yates rushed over to them and fluttered about as Sully helped Elizabeth to her feet, then gave them both hugs, inquiring about their ordeal and herding everyone, including the firemen, into the kitchen for the tea she'd never had a chance to make earlier.

Sully didn't let Elizabeth go even once, gathering her onto his lap when they sat down at the table, using the somewhat plausible excuse of there not being enough chairs to go around. The men didn't even crack grins— well, much anyway. They were learning.

She didn't protest, burrowing up against his chest and sipping her tea quietly as the conversation swirled around her. A feeling of overwhelming protectiveness swept over Sully as he held her there in his arms. He would do anything to keep her safe from harm. *Anything.* He would not have wanted to go on if Peel had—

Mais, non. He wasn't going to borrow despair. He'd stopped Peel, and the arsonist would soon be behind bars. He'd never bother either of them again.

"Let's go home," he said to Elizabeth after the big red

fire engine had driven away from Rose Cottage and he'd made sure Mrs. Yates would be all right alone.

Again that word, home, crept under his skin as he bussed Mrs. Yates on the cheek and told her to lock up after them. He took a backward glance at the plantation house as Elizabeth pointed the Corvette down the oyster shell path toward the village.

How lucky Tyree was. How nice it would be to have a place such as this to come home to at night, a loyal friend like Mrs. Yates to make sure all ran smoothly and a wife like Clara to share his life and his bed.

Non. A wife like Elizabeth.

Wife…

Did he really love her that much? Enough to marry her and spend the rest of this new, precious life with her?

Before when he'd asked her to stay in Magnolia Cove with him, he hadn't meant it like that. Hadn't intended to make things permanent. At least not until he was sure of his feelings. But now…was he sure?

Aye, he was. He *did* love her that much. Almost losing her to a madman had shown him how much she meant to him.

But what of her feelings for him? Did she feel the same way?

His heart sank. She may. Instinctively he felt she did. But she would never allow those emotions to flourish as long as she had to choose between him and her brother. Sully would lose every time.

But how could he betray his promise to his mother and father and his own sister, to avenge their cruel fates?

Should he agree to be tested and pray he wasn't a

match? His doctor said that chances were slim he'd be compatible even though he was related to Caleb. If he wasn't, it would solve the whole problem.

But what if he was? He had to face that possibility. And be ready to decide the boy's fate. Could Elizabeth ever forgive him for condemning her brother to death knowing he had the ability to save him?

Could Sully forgive himself?

Because of his own background, he'd always championed women, children and the helpless. Always.

But this particular child, this seed of his reviled enemy and murderer of his father and mother, did Sully have it in him to champion this one?

Le Bon Dieu, mait le main. God help him decide, for he surely could not.

Sully was being awfully quiet, staring pensively out the 'Vette's passenger window. To be honest, Elizabeth didn't feel much like talking herself.

What an ordeal! Being held at gunpoint had turned her legs to rubber and her heart into a locomotive.

Sully had been amazing. The look in his eyes as she was being held captive had been savage, brutal. There wasn't a doubt in her mind he would have given his life to save hers without a second thought. If Peel had as much as broken her skin he'd be dead now.

It was a little frightening, having a man be willing to die for you. There was something primitive, primal even, about that kind of a bond between a man and a woman. Something that would normally bind you together for life.

What was it about the Sullivans that was so terrible it prevented Sully from fulfilling the full promise of their bond?

She needed to know.

She needed to know where she stood.

"Sully?"

"Aye?"

"Can we make a stop before we go back to the Inn?"

"Sure. Where?"

"I'd like to go to your grave."

Fifteen minutes later, they were wandering along a cool shaded path in the Magnolia Cove Cemetery. Sully hadn't wanted to come, Elizabeth knew that. He'd argued and gotten mulish, then finally thrown up his hands and said, *"Bon."*

Hell, she wasn't sure she wanted to come, either. But she had to do it. Had to put herself into a mindset, an environment, where she could listen objectively to his answer when she asked the question that burned like acid in her heart.

Walking slowly under huge live oak trees that dripped with long strands of Spanish moss, they roamed through a quaint conglomeration of weathered headstones and past small, ornate wrought-iron family enclosures. The ancient brick pathway meandered lazily, giving them the opportunity to read the names and varied inscriptions, testaments to the lives and loves and connections of the people buried beneath. Every once in a while, Sully made a wistful noise of recognition.

It must be so strange for him knowing that every

human being alive during his past lifetime now reposed under a headstone somewhere.

For herself, Elizabeth had never liked graveyards. Not since her parents' funeral when she was a child. This one, being mainly historical, was thankfully different in character from the modern acres of pristine grass and pines where her parents slept. But it still gave her the creeps, in an unsettling, depressing way.

Why on earth had she insisted they come?

It was ridiculously morbid to want to look upon the grave of her lover. But she had to do it. She had to understand what he was going through, understand his past life in order to understand what drove his decisions about her and Caleb.

She would not go all Percy Shelley and ponder the bigger picture. She would not allow herself to wonder about the forces that had brought Sully back to life. Such things were far greater than she, and trying to grasp them would only end in futility.

But she would like to know *why* he'd come back.

Because she had enough faith that she firmly believed for such a miracle to occur, there must be a very good reason. If she could just find out what it was, she might be able to convince him that saving Caleb was part of that reason.

The pathway took a bend, and as they rounded it, they came face-to-face with...

"Merde," Sully swore softly. *"Sacre..."*

She stared in disbelief. Good Lord was right.

A large black wrought-iron enclosure surrounded two giant windswept-marble headstones, one for

Sullivan Fouquet and one for Elizabeth Hayden, engraved with names and dates. Below the lettering sailed a pair of ships, the hulls of which contained a different kind of writing.

She walked up to the enclosure and peered in for a closer look. The writing was two poems. The one on Sully's headstone read:

> No vow to God or girl or friend
> Could keep this gallant from his fate
> For Death leaves port without a sail
> Its driving breeze a cruel betrayal

"How ironic," he muttered, startling her. She hadn't realized he'd come up next to her. "That the real betrayal came from the woman they placed next to me."

She steeled her spine and turned to Elizabeth Hayden's marker.

> Ne'er a chance to be a bride
> For swiftly came life's changing tide
> Beauty and charm, her virtues exalted
> In the arms of her love her voyage was halted

She gritted her teeth at the saccharine lines. What. Ever.

Sully let out a derisive snort. "If she were still alive she'd not hold a candle to you, you know that, don't you?"

Her pique deflated. How could she be jealous when he said things like that?

"I can't believe they planted me next to the deceitful wench."

She turned to him and relaxed her jaw, giving him a gentle smile. "This isn't you, Sully. Not anymore. Let it go. Let it all go. You're not living in the past any longer. You're in the future now. Look forward, not back."

His mouth thinned and he took on a faraway look. "Easier said than done, *chère*. There are things—" He shook his head, turned and paced a few steps away, shoving his hands in his pockets.

At her insistence, on the way they had stopped at the Pirate's Rest to cut a bouquet of roses, which she carried on her arm. To give him some space, she lifted the latch of the gate and went into the enclosure, placing the flowers in a large glass vase hanging in a built-in wrought-iron holder on Sully's gravestone, next to the poem. Mrs. Butterfield had said there would also be a watering can filled with fresh water sitting behind the headstones, and sure enough, it was there. While they were cutting the flowers, Mrs. B had explained how Sullivan Fouquet had lots of admirers among the droves of pirate-obsessed tourists who found their way to Magnolia Cove, and that the Magnolia Cove Pirate Museum took care of the graves and made sure there was always fresh water available. The famous Cajun captain, after all, was the tiny village's one big claim to fame and its main tourist draw.

"Thought you were going to put those on the grave of your namesake," Sully drawled from behind her.

"Changed my mind," she said.

He gave her a wry smile and glanced at the mound of his grave with distaste. "Wishing I were still in there?"

She sucked in a breath. "Don't even joke like that, Sully."

He opened the gate for her. "Why are we here, *chère?*"

She walked over to an iron bench that sat under a nearby gnarled oak and took a seat. "We need to talk."

"Here? It feels rather ghoulish to have a tête-à-tête with one's lover at the foot of your own grave."

An involuntary shudder skittered up her spine, but she forced herself to remain sitting. "Yes, here. It seems somehow appropriate."

He pursed his lips and sat next to her. "*Bon.* And what would you like to talk about?"

"It's tomorrow, Sully. I lived up to my end of the bargain. Now it's your turn."

He shot to his feet again, glaring down at her. "*Your end of the bargain?* Are you… Are you trying to tell me last night was—"

"No," she interrupted. "That's not what I meant at all. But you asked me to stay and I did."

"And it was such a hardship?"

She bit her lip, quelling the aching in her heart. No, the hardship would come *after* having stayed, when she had to leave.

She sighed. "Sit down, Sully. It's time for you to tell me why you despise the Sullivans."

Chapter 15

Elizabeth watched Sully's handsome face darken and his expressive eyes narrow and take on the glitter of hatred. "Lizzie, are you sure you want to do this?" he asked, his voice low and rough with intensity.

She knew what was at stake. They obviously both did.

This would be either the end or the beginning. The place where their future was decided. He'd tell his story and either he'd draw a line in the sand and make her choose which side she would stand on, or she would be able to coax him to forgive, and erase it.

"Yes," she said. "We can't go on like this. I'm going home tomorrow. I want you to come with me, stay with me there, make a home together."

His lips parted and his eyes filled with an emotion

she couldn't decipher. "A home? On the Sullivan estate?" At the corner of his lip, a muscle jumped.

She nodded. "Or there's a village nearby. We could find an apartment."

She was laying out all her cards and it was terrifying. But she didn't care about her pride, or propriety or anything else. She loved him. She wanted him with her. The future? No one knew what the future would bring. Nothing had taught her that more poignantly than this trip to Magnolia Cove.

If he rejected her, so be it. But she wouldn't lose him for lack of trying.

He pushed out a breath and sat next to her, putting his elbows to his knees and staring out at his grave. He sat like that for a long time, until she was sure he didn't mean to answer.

Then finally he began to speak.

"The Acadians were treated like slaves, you know. Because of the political turmoil with France, in 1755 the British confiscated our lands in Nova Scotia and sold us as indentured servants to the highest bidder to pay for our own deportation. Some were lucky and escaped with just the shirts on their backs and made their way south along the coast, eventually settling down, mostly in Louisiana but in other places, too."

"I didn't know that," she said. "About being sold."

"Standard British procedure. Same deal with Australia. They pretended it wasn't slavery, but it was pretty damn close. You could work off your indenture after a certain number of years, theoretically. But if the master

wanted to keep you… Anyway, my parents landed with
Lord Henry Sullivan in Connecticut."

"Caleb's ancestor."

"And Andre Sullivan's, too." He gave a humorless
laugh. "Yet another irony."

"What happened?"

"Less than a year later, I was born. Three years after
that, my sister."

Her heart ached for him, guessing what was
coming next.

"Apparently old Lord Henry had taken an immedi-
ate shine to my mother. I found out later he'd raped
her repeatedly over the years. But what could she do?
Being indentured, she couldn't leave and accusations
against the master would only have made her ordeal
worse. So she hid her shame from her family and
lived with it."

The stark reality of his words, of his mother's suffering brought tears to her eyes. "Oh, Sully. I'm so sorry."

"None of us knew." He hung his head. "Maybe my
father knew in his heart. But one day he came home from
the fields and found his wife— Found that bastard—"

He swallowed heavily and she wanted to reach out
to him, to take him in her arms and rock him until the
hurt went away. She took his clenched hand in hers and
whispered unsteadily, "It's okay."

"No," he ground out. "It's not okay. My father went
crazy. Attacked him. Tried to kill him, like any normal
man would do under the circumstances. But the foreman
came running and dragged my father off him."

Elizabeth's blood screamed through her veins, not

wanting to hear what came next. She had an awful feeling…

"They hanged him. They took him straight to that big oak tree in front of the estate house and strung him up. No trial. No mercy. I remember my mother screaming, pleading for his life. That's when I found out I was Sullivan's bastard son."

She put her hands over her mouth to keep from crying out. Her eyes overflowed. *Oh, my God.* "I'm sorry. I'm so sorry."

He gave her a pitiless glance. "It gets better. When my father stopped moving at the end of the rope, my mother couldn't face life without him. She grabbed a knife from the belt of a man standing next to her and stabbed herself in the heart. I didn't notice because I was too busy fighting three of Lord Henry's thugs, trying to get to that oak tree to help my father. Not until I heard my little sister's wrenching sobs did I turn and see I'd lost both my parents that day."

Tears ran down Elizabeth's face as her heart broke in two. She couldn't say she was sorry again, because her throat was completely blocked by a huge lump of shame and horror that something so awful could have happened to him. To the family he loved. To anyone. She wanted to cover her ears, not listen to any more.

"Then, since I was branded a danger to society, I was tied behind a horse and dragged to the village jail to await transport to Louisiana to be with 'my kind.' I found out later that my sister had been sold to a family moving out west. She ended up in Kansas." He looked up and she saw the barest glimmer of a smile. "Clara, Tyree's wife, is her descendant."

A small sob escaped from deep inside Elizabeth at that unexpected happy twist in such a tragic tale.

Then another, larger one, escaped because she understood with dead certainty that never in a million years would he ever forgive the Sullivans for what they did to his family. Nor should he.

She rose from the bench, unable to speak, unable to do anything but shake her head and let the tears fall freely. She turned to flee. And was halted by his low, unsteady voice.

"Elizabeth. There's more."

She turned back to him, desperate to go, unable to bear it any longer. How could there possibly be more?

"You asked me once why I'd come back," he said. "Do you remember?"

She nodded, and all at once the pieces fell together and she understood that, as well. "Revenge," she shuddered out. "On the Sullivans."

He nodded grimly. "You were right about the voudou. It is what brought me back to life."

"The curse on Tyree?" she asked hoarsely, wishing, hoping that was it. Knowing it wasn't.

He rose and walked over to her, reached up and gathered her face in his hands. "*Non*. Not that one. When I was young and angry I put a curse on Lord Henry, on all his legitimate heirs. I cursed them to oblivion and begged to be alive to witness the demise of the Sullivan line."

The demise— She sucked in a breath of anguish. "Caleb!" she cried.

He nodded, looking oddly regretful. "The last two

male descendants of Lord Henry were Andre Sullivan and Caleb. Now there is just one left."

She could barely breathe. *Oh, God. Oh, my God.* "And you're here to see him die."

And she had thought Sully could cast a spell to *save* Caleb! Tears flooded anew.

"I'm sorry, Lizzie. Even if I took that blood test you want, I doubt I'd be a match. And if I were…" His words trailed off. "The curse is a powerful one, Elizabeth. There's nothing I can do."

So Caleb was fated to die because of Sully's quest to see the Sullivan line wiped from the earth. His revenge on Lord Henry would then be complete.

She looked at him through her veil of tears, and in his gaze saw a hint of regret, a hint of pride and a wellspring of pain and sorrow.

"I understand," she whispered.

And the worst part of it, the very worst part of all, was that she truly did.

Sully put his arm around Elizabeth's shoulders and together they walked back to the Pirate's Rest Inn. Somewhere along the line today he'd forgotten his stick, so they took it slow. They both used the time to pull themselves together. Not that he was in any hurry to get there. He dreaded what was to come. He dreaded the inevitable.

Which he had brought upon himself.

They arrived at the Inn and Mrs. Butterfield made a huge fuss. She'd heard all about what had happened at Rose Cottage. The news of Peel's capture had streaked around the village like wildfire, so they had to bank their personal crisis and sit and tell her all about it over more tea and crumpets. She must have attributed Sully's pensiveness and Elizabeth's red-rimmed eyes to the ordeal.

When they were finally able to escape the kitchen, they went up and Sully lay quietly on Elizabeth's bed, staring at the ceiling while she moved wordlessly around the room, packing her cases to leave for home in the morning. When she was finished, he heard her set them by the door. She was silent, but he felt her gaze on him.

"Elizabeth, I just want you to know—"

"Don't," she interrupted softly. "Please, Sully, whatever it is, either I already know or I can't bear to hear it."

He rolled his head on the pillow to see her standing in the middle of the room looking lost and forlorn and sadder than he'd ever seen anyone in his life. Her beautiful blue eyes glistened with unshed tears.

He nodded reluctantly, granting her that small comfort. Why put her through it—why put both of them through it?—making declarations of love and regret that would do neither any good?

He had wanted to tell her how much he loved her. How all this was tearing him apart from the inside out. How, if he had his life to live over again, if he could change that single thing, omit the curse on Lord Henry…the very thing that had brought him back to life…

He blew out a breath. Would he?

Would he change it if he could? Would he save the boy, knowing that by doing so he would lose the woman he loved? Lose this new chance at a good life, to lie instead forever in a grave next to the one who betrayed him?

Mon Dieu, the Devil's choice.

"Sully?"

"Aye?"

"Can we go to your room? This one is too depressing."

He tried to muster a smile. "Of course. How about a bath?"

Her attempt to smile was as unsuccessful as his. "That sounds nice."

So they went up to his room and stepped out of their clothes and ran a warm, fragrant bubble bath. He pulled her into his lap and they soaked together, her back nestled against his chest, for a long, long time. Not speaking, just being together. She tried to hide it, but he knew she wept again. And if truth be told, the moisture clinging to his own cheeks was not just from the tub.

They stayed until the water grew cold, then dried each other off. Neither felt like eating, so they climbed into the big, four-poster canopy bed and he held her in his arms and kissed her hair until finally she turned her face toward him and met his lips.

They made love—sad, tender, desperate love. They didn't talk. There was nothing left to say. They let their bodies speak for them.

And her body told him she didn't want to let him go.

His didn't, either.

But when the phone rang, waking them in the early hours of the morning, he knew their time had run out.

"I need to speak with Elizabeth," her mom's worried voice said. "It's Caleb. He's back in the hospital."

Elizabeth adjusted her airline seat all the way back and closed her eyes, struggling to hold in her chaotic emotions.

She'd managed to keep it together so far. It hadn't been easy.

The hour taxi ride to the Charleston airport had been strained at best. Sully had insisted on going with her, but had no clue about taxis or freeways or airports or airplanes. He'd been skeptical when she'd informed him she would be riding in one of those silver specks in the sky, and plain horrified when he'd actually seen one take off as they drove up to the terminal.

She didn't know whether to laugh or cry. In the end, she told the taxi to wait for him, checked her bags and gave him a long hug goodbye at security, shushing him so he wouldn't make a scene for not being able to go any farther with her and get himself arrested.

He told her to call him. She promised she would. Then he gave her one last kiss and let her go, looking nearly as miserable and abandoned as she felt.

She didn't look back. She couldn't. But now she wished she had. For just one more glimpse of the man she would always love.

Her Prius was waiting for her in the Connecticut airport parking lot, so she drove straight to the hospital, rushed to Caleb's room and gingerly opened the door.

His frail body lay under a bright white sheet, barely making a bump. He turned and greeted her with a tired but happy smile. "Bethy, you're here! But what about your vacation?"

She sat on the edge of the bed and grasped his hand, still battling to keep it together. "Oh, sweetie, I wasn't having any fun anyway. I wanted to come back and be with you. This is where I belong."

"I'm glad you came home," he said, and moved his head to look around her. "So, where is he?"

"Who, honey?"

"The man," he said, and gazed back at her hopefully. "The man Mama said you were in love with."

And that's when she burst into tears.

Sully poured himself another shot from the bottle of rum he'd had the taxi stop to pick up on the way back from the airport. Tossing it back, he slammed the glass onto the nightstand and paced back to the window of his room at the Pirate's Rest Inn. Outside, the afternoon sun reflected off the ever-moving surface of the inlet, glittering blue and gold. But today, even gazing out at the sea he loved so well could not cheer him.

For he was missing something else he loved even more. Elizabeth.

With a roar of frustration, he turned and paced back to the bottle. He'd had too much already, but it hadn't deadened the feelings of despair and anguish that had burned in his heart since she flew out of his life just hours before.

Would it ever get better?

The phone rang. He spun and swiped it up. *"Elizabeth?"*

"Sully, old man!"

After a second of confusion he burst out, "Tyree!"

"None other, my friend. Did I just hear something about Elizabeth?" His friend's voice was incredulous.

Sully groaned. *"Mon Dieu, mon ami.* You are not going to believe what's happened."

"Try me."

So he did. He told Tyree everything, from his and Elizabeth's first meeting in the garden, to sending her off in an airplane three hours ago. When he was finished, Tyree was silent for a few seconds, then he started to laugh.

Fury bubbled up in Sully. *What the—* "Are you insane? This is no laughing matter!"

"Ah, but it is, my friend. I am laughing because you have finally met a woman who is worthy of your love. Your single-minded, lifetime-loyal, all-obsessive love. It's about damn time."

"But I can't have her!" Sully snapped, feeling more like an ill-tempered child than a notorious sea captain who could make men tremble with a single glance.

"Who says?" Tyree asked.

"She does," he answered, his anger crashing into wretched misery.

"But I thought she asked you to live with her, build a home together. Doesn't sound to me like she's the problem."

Sully pressed his lips together in frustration. "*Caleb* is the problem. She won't have me unless I try to save her brother."

"Are you sure?"

"Damn it, man, of course I'm sure!"

There was a pause, as though his friend doubted him. Sully wanted to reach through the blasted phone line and shake the man.

"Do you love her?"

"Tyree, the boy is a Sullivan. How can I possibly help him?"

"Do you love her?"

"And what about the voudou curse? There's nothing I can do about that!"

"But, do you *love* her?"

"Yes, damn you, I love her!" he shouted desperately.

"Well, then," Tyree said evenly. "There's your answer."

What the hell was that supposed to mean?

Sully tried to press him further, but Tyree deliberately changed the subject and refused to go back to it, saying Sully had to figure out what was best all on his own.

Then Clara came on the line, too, and they regaled him with stories of the adventures they'd shared together thus far in their year-long sail around the world. By the time they hung up, Sully was green with envy over the trip, over their good fortune to be together and over their obvious love for one another.

Tyree loved Clara so much he would have moved heaven and earth to be with her. Hell, he *did* move heaven and earth and he lived through two centuries in limbo to find and be with her. In the end he'd even been willing to die for her love.

Did Elizabeth deserve any less from Sully?

Did Sully even deserve her love if he wasn't willing to sacrifice everything to be with her? *Everything?*

Was that what Tyree meant when he'd asked if Sully loved her? And that his answer alone should tell him what he needed to do?

He *did* love her.

And suddenly Sully understood.

Love. Love was the miracle that had brought him back to life, not revenge.

Was he such a fool as to throw away something as precious as his love for Elizabeth and her love for him, for the sake of that hollow, empty reward? A revenge that was bitter and meaningless at best?

Love was the most important thing a man could have. His parents had died for it. For each other. And if Sully lost Elizabeth, it was Henry Sullivan who will have triumphed in the end, his poison having spread even to this distant time and place.

Elizabeth was right. He had been brought back for a reason. And now he saw that reason clearly.

But he must act. Soon.

Before it was too late.

Elizabeth felt a little better after getting something into her stomach. She hadn't eaten since…she couldn't remember. Between all the trauma yesterday and skipping dinner last night and breakfast this morning, who knew? But this evening her mom had recognized the signs of near collapse and sent her down to the hospital cafeteria while Gilda and Caleb watched their favorite reality show.

Food had helped. Elizabeth's body, anyway. Her mind…

Not so good.

After her mortifying breakdown in front of Caleb, she'd run to the rest room and cried herself out. When she returned to his hospital room afterward, both her mom and brother had tried to find out what was wrong. But she didn't want to talk about it. She didn't want to think about it.

Sully was gone from her life and she had to accept that.

So when she walked into Caleb's room and saw Sully standing there by the bed talking to him, she didn't believe her eyes.

In fact, she fainted.

When she awoke, she was in Sully's arms and he was carrying her across the hall to an empty bed.

"No," she protested, her mind clawing through the stars and the sharp smell of ammonia. "Please. I don't want to leave Caleb."

The nurse who was leading them frowned, and her mom, who was clutching her dangling hand and looking anxious, said, "But darling, you need to—"

"No, Mom." She smiled and adjusted herself in Sully's arms. Still not daring to look at him, lest he morph into a hospital orderly or security guard and prove she really was losing it. "I'm fine, Mom. Really. It's just—" Just what? Excitement? Voudou? PTSD? "Jet lag," she said lamely.

Both the nurse and her mom dissolved into portraits of doubt, but Caleb called out, "She can lie down next to me for a few minutes. I'll make room."

Sully reversed directions. As he did so she felt him lean down and press a kiss to her forehead. She put her nose to his throat and the scent of him inundated her senses, banishing all other smells, and she knew with comforting certainty she wasn't hallucinating. It really was him.

She took a deep, shuddering breath and met his eyes.

He smiled. "Hi."

She fought the emotions that flooded through her at seeing him. And she fought the seemingly endless font of tears that prickled.

"Hi," she said. It was all she could manage without losing the battle.

"I flew in an airplane," he said, his eyes crinkling at the edges.

A half-sob half-laugh escaped her. "You did?" After all the anxiety and trepidation over *her* flying... He must have been— "Oh, dear. The poor stewardess."

"Steward, actually." He came to a halt beside Caleb's bed. "I told him it was my first time. I think it turned him on," he added in a whisper. She giggled, but clutched his neck desperately when he tried to lower her. "Don't want to lie down, *chère?*"

"No." She didn't want to let go of him. If she let go maybe he would disappear again. Maybe she was still unconscious and dreaming all this, his reassuring smell and all.

"D'accord." He sat down on the edge of the bed instead, still holding her in his arms. She held on to him for dear life.

Caleb broke the awkward silence. "He's the one, isn't he?" he said enthusiastically. "See, you didn't have to be so sad. I knew he'd come for you."

Elizabeth gave a watery smile at his youthful naiveté. "And how did you know that, Squirt?"

Caleb grinned. "Because if he hadn't, I'd have called him up and *made* him come for you. No one gets to make my sister sad!"

Elizabeth glanced up to see Sully's lips twist in a somber smile. "That's right, Caleb," he said. "Brothers are supposed to protect their sisters."

There was a commotion at the door, and the nurse

spoke a few words to someone, then a different nurse came in looking all efficient and holding a cloth-covered tray.

"Here we are, Mr. Sullivan." She stopped and took in Elizabeth sitting on his thighs. A disapproving frown appeared on her face. "Except you seem to be busy."

"Not *that* busy. Here." He lifted his less-occupied arm and shook it out. "Use this one."

"What's going on?" Elizabeth said, looking from the nurse to him, and then, stunned, to the hypodermic needle she unveiled on the tray.

"Sully came to be my donor!" Caleb piped up cheerfully. "He said he's my cousin so we might be a match! He said maybe not, but he'd try real hard to be one."

Her mom walked over to take Caleb's hand, nodding happily when Elizabeth darted a confused glance at her for confirmation.

"Sully arrived while you were in the cafeteria. Introduced himself and said he wanted to be tested."

Elizabeth could scarcely believe it. Joy flooded through her whole being. He'd changed his mind! "But…I don't understand. How can you forgive…"

His smile turned gentle as he held his arm out for the nurse to stick. "I love you, Elizabeth, and nothing's going to keep me from being with you. Nothing."

Her composure crumbled. She was beginning to feel like a fountain she couldn't turn off, but she just couldn't help herself. She buried her face in his shirt and just cried. For happiness. For Caleb. For Sully's mother and father. For the sheer love of the man who held her in his arms.

"That's you, then," she heard the efficient nurse tell

Sully. "Bend your elbow. That's right. Now. How about you, young lady? Have you had a test yet?"

She glanced up and wiped the flood from her cheeks. "Yes. I'm afraid I'm not a match."

The nurse waved her hand, as though her answer were a pesky fly. "Don't mean that kind. I mean—" She flicked a quick glance at Caleb and pursed her lips. "You know. A *test*."

"I'm afraid I'm not—"

"You fainted, didn't you? And, well, to put it bluntly, are you usually this hormonal? Tell me, do you have any tenderness…anywhere?"

There was an explosive pause.

"Oh, my goodness," her mom breathed. "Darling, are you—"

But Elizabeth didn't hear the rest of the question because she'd finally deciphered the nurse's meaning and her head started spinning again. She gasped.

"What is she talking about?" Sully asked, his voice filled with concern. "What are hormones?"

She stared up at him, her mind blazing through the times they'd… "Oh, my God," she whispered. The last time, that last night, they were both so upset they'd forgotten. And now she thought about it, maybe the time before that, too…

"She's going to have a baby!" Caleb cried out, grinning like a Cheshire cat. "Yippee! I'm going to be an uncle!"

"Caleb!" their mom admonished, turning an embarrassed shade of pink.

He looked triumphant. "Thank goodness! I thought I'd never get you married off so Mama can have grandkids." Then his sweet little face faltered. He peered apprehensively at her, then at Sully. "You two are married, aren't you?"

Sully looked like he'd seen a ghost. There was dead silence in the room for a moment, then he cleared his throat and found his voice. "We will be soon, Caleb. And we'll be honored to make you an uncle." It was Sully's turn to falter. "That is—" He looked down at her, a thousand emotions running through his expressive brown eyes. "If you'll have me, after…everything I put you through."

But the one emotion that shone there brighter than all the rest was devotion. To her.

Her heart simply melted.

"Of course I will," she whispered, all the love in her heart bubbling up and overflowing for this amazing man who was willing to give up so much for her. "I love you, too, Sully. More than you'll ever know. And nothing will ever make me happier than being under your spell forever."

Epilogue

Two years later…

Sully leaned back contentedly in his deck chair and gazed out across the marshy inlet behind his house, watching the fiery red and yellow orb of the sun slip slowly below the horizon. A soft, warm breeze rustled the sea oats and gracefully swayed the spartina grass, making ripples in the still waters that stretched in a half-moon around them. He squeezed Elizabeth's hand, who was reclining on the chair next to him. Another perfect end to another perfect day.

Below the deck where they were sitting, beyond the jumble of the riotous flower beds and a stretch of lush green grass, their son, Jack, toddled onto their long jetty, his pudgy little right hand clutching Gilda's, his left gripping his uncle Caleb's. They were all laughing as they ran onto the jetty, headed for the *Clara Elizabeth.*

"Uh-oh," Tyree said with a chuckle from the porch swing where he sat cuddled with his wife, Clara, who more sprawled than sat next to him. "You don't think your mother-in-law is going out there to check on our progress, do you?"

Sully grinned. The *Clara Elizabeth* was the sleek old sailboat he and Tyree were spending the summer restoring. But for some reason, between the sun and the ale and the crab traps and fishing poles—not to mention the amiable company—not a lot of headway had been made on the work lately. Shoot, the guys from the fire station kept dropping by and Tyree kept having to run up to the house to check on his eight-month-pregnant wife, and Elizabeth kept bringing Jack down to see his daddy, and Caleb kept asking ten million questions about sailing and carpentry and the proper way to hold a crab line and a thousand other things. The poor kid had led a sheltered life up there in Connecticut.

"What's a man to do?" Sully said with an expansive shrug. "We needed dinner and neither of us felt like going to the store. Feeding our families comes first."

From Tyree's lap came Clara's eloquent snort.

Next to him, Elizabeth laughed softly. "I'm telling you, Sully, *you're* the one who gets to tell Mom it won't be ready to take her sailing before she leaves for Connecticut at the end of the summer."

"It'll be ready," he assured her with a wince. *Maybe.*

"Besides, I was thinking of asking her and Caleb to stay. How dumb is it to go back up north for the winter?"

Elizabeth's mouth opened in pleased surprise. "Really?"

"The house is plenty big enough. Why not?"

"What about the farm?"

He took a deep breath. He'd spent a couple of months there while donating bone marrow to Caleb, and after, as the boy had slowly recovered. It had changed a lot since Sully lived there as a boy himself. The old oak tree was gone. Thank God. He didn't think he could have taken seeing it again. But it was now a completely different place. And he'd made peace with it, with the events that had transpired there. He'd let it go.

"I'm sure the family we hired to take care of it for the summer would stay on."

"You wouldn't sell it, would you?" she asked quietly.

"*Non.* It belongs to Caleb," he said. "It's his heritage."

"And Andre Sullivan's. And yours. Yours more than anyone."

He smiled at her, his beautiful, wise, understanding wife. "Have I told you lately how much I love you, Elizabeth Sullivan?"

"Not for at least the last hour," she said, her adoring smile meeting his.

Dieu, he had to be the luckiest man on earth.

"Come here," he said, and pulled her onto his lap for a long kiss.

From deep in the porch swing came a long-suffering groan from Clara. "They're at it again, aren't they?"

Tyree chuckled. "'Fraid so, sweeting."

"Lord, Lizzie," Clara groaned in a warning voice, "keep doing that and you'll end up looking like me!" She moaned dramatically, holding her huge belly.

Sully looked at Elizabeth and raised his brows suggestively. She tipped her head and waggled hers back at him.

That was all the invitation he needed.

He swept her up in his arms and headed for the French doors off the deck. "Call us when supper's ready," he told Tyree, who started to laugh.

"What should we name this one?" Elizabeth whispered as he lowered her onto their big, welcoming four-poster bed.

"How about Genevieve?" he quietly said, his heart so full of love it felt close to bursting. "After my mother."

Elizabeth's smile shone back at him. The smile that lit up his life and gave him more joy than he'd ever known possible. "I do love you, Sullivan Fouquet," she whispered. "And I will till the end of time."

And he knew it was true. That they were destined to be together forever, a magical enchantment holding them together so strongly they could never be torn apart, no matter which way the winds of destiny blew. The greatest magical enchantment of all.

Love.

* * * * *

Gwen took a taxi to the Yellow Parrot, and with each passing block she grew more tense. It didn't take a rocket scientist to figure out that this dive was in the worst part of town. Gwen had learned to take care of herself, but the minute she entered the bar, she realized that a smart woman would have brought a gun with her. The interior was hot, smelly and dirty, and the air was so smoky that it looked as if a pea soup fog had settled inside the building. Before she had gone three feet, an old drunk came up to her and asked for money. Side-stepping him, she searched for someone who looked as if he or she might actually work here, someone other than the prostitutes who were trolling for customers.

After fending off a couple of grasping young men and ignoring several vulgar propositions in an odd mix-

ture of Spanish and English, Gwen found the bar. She
ordered a beer from the burly, bearded bartender. When
he set the beer in front of her, she took the opportunity
to speak to him.

"I'm looking for a man. An older American man, in
his seventies. He was probably with a younger woman.
This man is my father and—"

"*No hablo inglés.*"

"Oh." He didn't speak English and she didn't speak
Spanish. Now what?

While she was considering her options, Gwen noticed a young man in skintight black pants and an open
black shirt, easing closer and closer to her as he made
his way past the other men at the bar.

Great. That was all she needed—some horny young
guy mistaking her for a prostitute.

"*Señorita.*" His voice was softly accented and slightly slurred. His breath smelled of liquor. "You are all
alone, *sí?*"

"Please, go away," Gwen said. "I'm not interested."

He laughed, as if he found her attitude amusing.
"Then it is for me to make you interested. I am Marco.
And you are…?"

"Leaving," Gwen said.

She realized it had been a mistake to come here
alone tonight. Any effort to unearth information about
her father in a place like this was probably pointless.
She would do better to come back tomorrow and try to
speak to the owner. But when she tried to move past her
ardent young suitor, he reached out and grabbed her
arm. She tensed.

Looking him right in the eyes, she told him, "Let go of me. Right now."

"But you cannot leave. The night is young."

Gwen tugged on her arm, trying to break free. He tightened his hold, his fingers biting into her flesh. With her heart beating rapidly as her basic fight-or-flight instinct kicked in, she glared at the man.

"I'm going to ask you one more time to let me go."

Grinning smugly, he grabbed her other arm, holding her in place.

Suddenly, seemingly from out of nowhere, a big hand clamped down on Marco's shoulder, jerked him back and spun him around. Suddenly free, Gwen swayed slightly but managed to retain her balance as she watched in amazement as a tall, lanky man in jeans and cowboy boots shoved her would-be suitor up against the bar.

"I believe the lady asked you real nice to let her go," the man said, in a deep Texas drawl. "Where I come from, a gentleman respects a lady's wishes."

Marco grumbled something unintelligible in Spanish. Probably cursing, Gwen thought. Or maybe praying. If she were Marco, she would be praying that the big, rugged American wouldn't beat her to a pulp.

Apparently Marco was not as smart as she was. When the Texan released him, he came at her rescuer, obviously intending to fight him. The Texan took Marco out with two swift punches, sending the younger man to the floor. Gwen glanced down at where Marco lay sprawled flat on his back, unconscious.

Her hero turned to her. "Ma'am, are you all right?"

She nodded. The man was about six-two, with a sun-burned tan, sun-streaked brown hair and azure-blue eyes.

"What's a lady like you doing in a place like this?" he asked.

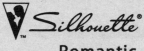

Romantic
SUSPENSE

Excitement, danger and passion guaranteed!

Same great authors and riveting editorial
you've come to know and love
from Silhouette Intimate Moments.

New York Times
bestselling author
Beverly Barton
is back with the
latest installment
in her popular
miniseries,
The Protectors.
HIS ONLY
OBSESSION
is available
next month from
Silhouette®
Romantic Suspense

Look for it wherever you buy books!

Visit Silhouette Books at www.eHarlequin.com   SRSBB27525

This February...

Catch NASCAR Superstar *Carl Edwards* in
SPEED DATING!

Kendall assesses risk for a living—
so she's the last person you'd
expect to see on the arm of a
race-car driver who thrives on the
unpredictable. But when a bizarre
turn of events—and NASCAR
hotshot Dylan Hargreave—inspire
her to trade in her ever-so-structured
existence for "life in the fast lane"
she starts to feel she might be
on to something!

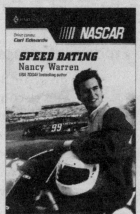

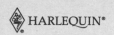

EVERLASTING LOVE™

Every great love has a story to tell™

Save $1.⁰⁰ off

the purchase of
any Harlequin
Everlasting Love novel

Coupon valid from January 1, 2007
until April 30, 2007.

Valid at retail outlets in the U.S. only.
Limit one coupon per customer.

RETAILER: Harlequin Enterprises Limited will pay the face value of this coupon plus 8¢ if submitted by the customer for this product only. Any other use constitutes fraud. Coupon is nonassignable. Void if taxed, prohibited or restricted by law. Consumer must pay any government taxes. Void if copied. For reimbursement submit coupons and proof of sales directly to: Harlequin Enterprises Ltd., P.O. Box 880478, El Paso, TX 88588-0478, U.S.A. Cash value 1/100¢. Valid in the U.S. only. ® is a trademark of Harlequin Enterprises Ltd. Trademarks marked with ® are registered in the United States and/or other countries.

5 65373 00076 2   (8100) 0 11302

HEUSCPN0407

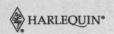

HARLEQUIN®

E V E R L A S T I N G L O V E ™

Every great love has a story to tell ™

Fall from Grace

Kristi Gold

Save $1.⁰⁰ off

the purchase of
any Harlequin
Everlasting Love novel

Coupon valid from January 1, 2007
until April 30, 2007.

Valid at retail outlets in Canada only.
Limit one coupon per customer.

52607370

HECDNCPN0407

REQUEST YOUR FREE BOOKS!

2 FREE NOVELS PLUS 2 FREE GIFTS!

Silhouette® Romantic

SUSPENSE

Sparked by Danger, Fueled by Passion!

Silhouette®

Romantic

SUSPENSE

COMING NEXT MONTH